Gold Mountain

Gold Mountain

Anne Azel

P.D. Publishing, Inc.
Clayton, North Carolina

ISBN-13: 978-1-933720-04-3
ISBN-10: 1-933720-04-2

9 8 7 6 5 4 3 2 1

Cover art by B.L. Magill
Cover design by Barb Coles
Edited by Day Petersen/Betty Anderson Harmon

Published by:

P.D. Publishing, Inc.
P.O. Box 70
Clayton, NC 27528

http://www.pdpublishing.com

Acknowledgements:

My thanks to Debra Butler for her support and hard work on my behalf and to Barb and Linda and all the PR staff for their outstanding efforts.

DEDICATION

To Jean.

Golden Mountain was the name that the Chinese people gave to the New World in the 1800s. Even in the homes of poverty, homes of red dust and little rice, they had heard of the Golden Mountain. If you could get papers and passage to the Golden Mountain, then you would return to China rich and help your family and village, and bring honour to the name of your ancestors. But first, you must bribe a lot of people for the proper papers and pay the five hundred dollar head tax. This was a suck-in-the-breath amount of money. Five hundred dollars was a year's wages for some, a lifetime's for others. Five hundred dollars was the Impossible Mountain. The Debt Mountain. The Theft Mountain. The Soul Lost Mountain.

In the 1800s, some men counted themselves lucky to get contracts to labour in the gold fields of California or build the thin railway lines lost in the vast open spaces that became a penetrating root that would spread across Canada and the United States of America. The railway would bring a steam infusion of settlers – an intrusion. The Chinese were indentured labourers, brought in only to work, and when the work was done they were to go home. But they didn't. They couldn't. They had no riches, only blisters. They dug to the heart of the Golden Mountain, but others claimed the wealth of their toil. They had no dreams left, no money, no honour, and so they stayed. They sent money back to their families when they could, and were buried far from their ancestors in the slag heaps left from their digging and their lives.

When cheap labourers were no longer needed, the governments of the New World tried their best to get rid of them. They were taking jobs from real Canadians and Americans – white immigrants. They established laws to prevent these broken, lonely men from bringing out wives, children, and other family. The head tax continued to rise. It was blood money.

My father was one of the few who came to the Golden Mountain in the early 1900s, when the head tax was very high. When he left China, he cut his pig tail and changed his name to Jimmy. Not James, just Jimmy. Jimmy Li. He opened a Chinese take-out in the back of a red brick building in the village of Cooksville. Cooksville would grow up to be an urban sprawl called Mississauga, a huge satellite city of Toronto, Ontario, Canada, but it was a crossroads village then. When I was young, the red brick building still had an old rusted ring in the wall where they had tethered the stagecoaches years before. My father was tethered to the building too. His take-out was always open, even on Christmas. The only day the take-out was closed was on my father's birthday. He first rented space in the red brick building, then bought the building, then bought other buildings that he rented to cover his mortgages. They were always red brick buildings, imperial buildings in my father's mind. My father would grow smaller, older, and richer each year.

My father was sixty-two years old when he had me. When I was young, I was embarrassed to have such an old father. I would tell my white Canadian friends that my real father was dead and Jimmy was my grandfather. Later, I was sort of proud that my father could conceive me at sixty-two. This was without enhancement drugs, you understand. My father conceived me under his own steam.

I cannot remember not being in the kitchen of our take-out. My mother cooked along with the others, her stomach round and full of hope. I was to be Jimmy's son. Once born, and a girl, I lay in a back corner of the kitchen in an old crib. I watched the activity intently as I sucked my hand and filled my diaper, fulfilling my role in the family while wrapped in the comfort of food smells and Chinese voices. I was a contented baby. I didn't know yet that I was a disappointment.

As I got older, I played in my back corner with dark serious eyes and an expressionless face. I knew by then I was a disappointment; my mother told me so often. "If you had been a son, your father would have married me," she would say as she combed my hair with strokes made hard by emotion and strong work hands. My mother was not my father's wife. His wife shared a room with my father; my mother had a room next to my half sister's and mine. My mother was my father's concubine.

He had met her in China when he had made his first trip back to his village after many years. She was the third daughter of an old school friend. My father would say he had not found her pretty, but she looked strong and healthy and so he thought she would give him the son his wife could not. First, he had made arrangements with her father and an agreed bride price was established. My father then took my mother for a walk in the vegetable garden. He did not talk of love; he talked of red brick buildings.

"I am a man of substance. I own a red brick building, but I am still poor because I have no son to carry on my family name. If you are willing to come to Canada and work hard and give me a son, I will make you my wife and you will have anything you want. If you do not have a son, you will work hard and I will provide for you."

My mother was a practical woman. As a third daughter, she had no prospects beyond marriage to some local farmer. Politically, China was not a good place to be. It was Red. Not red brick, but red Maoist and Red Guard. My father, she knew, was educated and kind. Even if he was old and wrinkled, his breath was still fresh. She would be better off with him in the Golden Mountain. And so, she had agreed.

I called my father's wife, Aunt Quin. My half sister is five years older than myself. She was called Sarah. I am Kelly. I am strong and healthy, like my mother. I am not pretty, but women say I am handsome.

1955 was the year of my father's happiness. He adopted a son. My father rented a big hall, and many people came to offer their congratulations. I was too young to question where my brother had come from or why he was not living with us. I do not know if my sister Sarah asked. If she did, I am sure she didn't get an answer. My mother would say, "We can't talk of these things. These people," she would say, "have never had to boil nettles and cut them to survive. They cannot understand." I had never had to survive on nettles, either, but I knew not to talk of things within the Chinese community to those on the outside. When I went to school, and later to work, I went through a cultural decompression chamber each morning and came out into the liquid white world, protected by a deep diving suit of secrets.

And so, after 1955, I had a half sister and brother. My brother's Chinese name meant The Noble One. His English name was Jason. Sarah and I had no Chinese names. My father thought for a long time about what my brother's name should be. Sarah and I were named by our mothers: Sarah, after Sarah Bernhardt, and me after Grace Kelly. I did not meet my brother until I was fourteen. He was raised in Singapore by relatives.

My first experience with a woman was also in 1955. I was five years old and my father had bought a TV. It was a black and white picture, and came in a wood cabinet that took up a whole corner of the room. Workmen came and put an antenna on the roof of our red brick building. My father went outside to look up at it. The antenna was another symbol of his success.

Sarah and I were not normally allowed to watch TV. My father watched. Sometimes his wife and my mother were allowed to watch, as well. My father watched wrestling and horse racing. He watched Gorgeous George and Man of War. He gambled on these events. Gambling is a Chinese vice. We are superstitious because we like to gamble. We look for signs, knock on wood, carry charms, anything that will bring us good Joss, good luck. My father was lucky at gambling, but not lucky at having sons, not until that year.

In 1955, Sarah and I were allowed to watch TV this one night. It was a special treat, because it was the year of my father's happiness. My mom and aunt made a special meal, and we were allowed

to stay up late to watch Mary Martin in *Peter Pan*. I was mesmer-
ized. I wanted to be Peter Pan, because I was too young to know
that I wanted Wendy. My sister wanted to be Wendy and have two
sons. That was one of the many differences between my sister and
myself. I was not afraid to fly across rainbows to Neverland to fight
pirates, and Sarah was not afraid to be tethered to a red brick building.

That was many years ago now. In a futile attempt to prove my
worth, I excelled in school and ended up fighting pirates in a court
of law. It was in court that I met Jane Anderson. I cross examined
her. She was the arresting officer, and I, the lawyer for the defen-
dant. My client was a Chinese Canadian businessman charged with
smuggling. I was looking for loopholes in order to save my guilty
client from jail time. I found none. My client got five years and a
bill from me for ten thousand. He could have gotten ten years and a
bill for fifteen thousand, but the courts, and I, were lenient.

I met Jane again three months later, at a climbing meet on
Hamilton Mountain. She scrambled past me and deliberately took
my next handhold. It would have been bad etiquette if she'd done it
out of carelessness, but doing it deliberately made it a challenge. I
followed her up and used my height to intimidate. I am tall for an
Oriental.

"You probably don't know this, but you don't cut off the ascent
of another climber."

"You probably don't know this, but the law is there to protect
society, not the guilty."

I remembered her then. Out of uniform and in a sweat stained
t-shirt, she was still worth noticing. "I was doing my job, which was
to defend my client, as is his right under the law."

"Glad I don't have your job." She let her line drop over the side
and rappelled down to a woman who waited for her at the bottom.

Even in those closeted days, I sensed they were a couple. I
coiled up my lines slowly, giving them time to move off. I am a good
lawyer; I had done nothing wrong. Still, I did not like the feeling
this cop's criticism had left inside me. I felt my comfort levels violated. *Screw the bitch*, I thought, and then smiled. I would have
liked to.

Our paths did not cross again for over a year, not until the night
of the accident. An officer from the police station phoned my condo
to tell me my mother was trapped in her car and was calling for me.
I drove like a lunatic to the scene of the accident, using my Crown
Attorney ID to get through the police line. I ran up to the over-
turned car and found Officer Anderson kneeling in the mud, holding
my mother's hand and talking to her softly as the paramedics

worked to stabilize her.

"So, what does your daughter do?" I heard her ask.

"I'm a lawyer," I said from behind her, and then knelt down by my mother and talked to her in Cantonese, ignoring Anderson. After a minute, Officer Anderson got up and moved off. We were even.

The night of the accident, my mother had taken the car to go to bingo at the Chinese Cultural Centre. She had gotten on the exit ramp, but had somehow managed to drift over to the shoulder of the road and roll down the embankment. Later, at the hospital, I would learn that she'd had a small stroke.

I'd always thought it would be my father who would die first. He was ninety-five and fragile, but still sat in his office and worked each day. My father never mixed business with pleasure. His mind was quick, and he still put in an eight hour day before turning on the news to get the race results. My mother was fifty-five, and was having strokes.

I sat at her side at the hospital and held her hand. She'd had another stroke on the way to the hospital, and she looked at me with blank eyes and made noises like a baby.

Reality is smoke from an incense stick: fragrant and varied, but elusive. We know who we are only until our mind wanders down new paths, then we are lost. I wondered what paths her mind was taking her down, and whether she would meet me there or would never recognize me again.

By morning, she knew me but she was confused and scared. She kept asking me why she was in a hospital and scolding me for not taking her to a Chinese doctor who knew the old medicines. It was several days before I was allowed to take her home. I explained to her that she had dangerously high blood pressure and would need to be on medication. I took her to my condo; Aunt Quin had enough to do with caring for my father. So, after living with my father for thirty-four years, she left him. She did not seem to mind, and neither did he. They now walked down different paths. Reality is smoke.

So my mother came to live with me after her accident and stroke. It was a daughter's duty to take care of her family. While I did not question this, I did resent it. I enjoyed my private world. I am, by nature, a solitary creature. What gay person has not lived in isolation? Since adulthood, I had lived a discreet but alternative life style. Having my mother move into my guest room was like moving home and being a child once more. I lost control. My Western frozen dinners disappeared and my apartment smelt of Eastern herbs and spices and things tossed in a wok. I was forced back to eating rice and giving up pizza.

I phoned Mom three times a day from my office and spent evenings with her. I spoilt her, and she spoilt me. One day, a week after I moved her in with me, she appeared at the door to my den. "Kelly." My name sounded foreign on my mother's lips. It was a very different sounding name when my friends said it. "You must find that nice cop who helped me. You must thank her and give her a gift. I have some red money envelopes. We will give her some money in thanks."

I smiled. In the Chinese culture, the gift of money is common. We have special red envelopes for such gifts. Sometimes the chop for good luck or good fortune is embossed in gold on the front. "I can't give a police officer money, Mom. It would be seen as a bribe."

My mother sniffed in annoyance. She felt that white Canadians were very strange. They would order Chinese food, but insist that it only be made with European ingredients. They would pick up the wrong fortune cookie, not knowing that the ends must be pointing towards them. And they would ask why there was no take-out rice pudding. Rice as a dessert; how ridiculous.

"Then you must give her another gift. It is proper. I will pay."

I was a child again. My mother had given me an order and I would obey. What kind of gift did one buy for a cop?

When I was in elementary school, students would give each other valentine cards. The teacher would have us make envelopes to stick on the side of our desks. They were our valentine mailboxes. We decorated them with red and pink hearts that we cut from construction paper and stuck on with mucilage. The teacher told us not to eat the glue because it was made from horse's hooves, and you never knew where a horse had been. I had a pretty good idea.

I never got a lot of cards, and I never knew what to do with the ones I did. These cards were bought in variety stores in sheets. All you had to do was punch out the cards and sign your name. Some said things like, "Roses are red, violets are blue, sugar is sweet and so are you." Others said things like, "Roses are red, cabbages are green, sugar is sweet and you're ugly and mean." Which were supposed to be funny and which were truth? Reality is smoke.

My mother let me buy my cards the night before Valentine's Day, when they were on sale. I was allowed to sit up late to get them done. I sent everyone in the class a valentine because I didn't like to hurt anyone's feelings. The ones I got, I took home and then secretly threw them out. More secrets. Even small secrets build up over time.

I did keep one card in fourth grade, from Tracy. She sat three seats over from me and giggled a lot. She was very popular and I was proud she had given me a card. I stuck it on the mirror above my dresser and left it there until spring. Then I threw it away. I cannot remember Tracy's last name, but I do remember she favoured pink underpants and liked to dance around in them in the girls' change room. My undies were always white, and I tried not to show them. I am a private person of many secrets.

I phoned police headquarters and found out that Officer Anderson worked out of Station Six. I phoned Station Six and left my cell phone number, requesting that Officer Anderson call me. She did, several days later.

"This is Officer Anderson. I have a message to call this number to speak to Kelly."

I took the call in my office, leaning back in my chair and trying to act as if I were in control. I did not feel in control. I was a little girl back in a red brick house, doing the chores my mother had set for me.

"Officer Anderson, this is Kelly Li, over at the Crown Attorney's Office."

"I thought you were in criminal law working for Barrs, Miller, and Wang."

"Now I work as a Crown Attorney."

"Welcome to the other side."

The remark had an edge of dry sarcasm to it that I ignored. "Last week my mother had a stroke and rolled her car. You were very kind to her and she wanted me to express her thanks."

"It was my job. How is she?"

"She had another stroke on the way to the hospital, but she seems to have recovered, although she is not as active as she has been in the past."

"I'm glad she is okay. She was scared."

"Yes, she would be."

"Thanks for calling. Please give your mother my best."

"There is something else."

"What?"

"My mother wants to give you a gift."

"Counsellor, you know better."

"Yes, but my mother doesn't. She wanted me to give you money; it is the Chinese way. I thought perhaps we could find some middle ground and I might be able to thank you by taking you to dinner."

"With you?"

She didn't need to sound so incredulous. I gritted my teeth. "Yes."

There was silence at the other end while she considered. "All right."

"Good. Are you free Saturday?"

"Yes."

"Where can I pick you up?"

"Let's meet somewhere."

"Very well. What do you like to eat?"

"Chinese."

Was she being funny? My silence must have alerted her to my annoyance.

"I figured you'd know a good place."

"Oh. Actually, I have a better idea where to buy good pizza."

She laughed.

Was I making progress in this chore? "I'll ask my mother. I'm sure she'll know a good place for American Chinese."

"American Chinese?"

"North Americans do not like real Chinese."

"How do you know?"

"My family runs a take-out."

"Is the food good?"

I got huffy. "Of course the food is good! What do you think we do, pick up stray cats on the street and stew them in sweet and sour sauce?"

She laughed again, not realizing how sensitive a subject this is. Do the Whites not realize that we know what they say about us?

"Okay, let's go get take-out at your place. I picked the place, so you pick the meal."

"Okay. Saturday at eight. Jimmy Li's Take-Out. It's the corner of Hurontario and Dundas. A red brick building."

"I know the place. Saturday, then. Thanks."

I phoned my mother to tell her I was taking Officer Anderson out for dinner on Saturday night.

"Where?" my mother wanted to know.

"Our place, in the kitchen."

We had been talking English, now there was an explosion of Cantonese. Officer Anderson would be insulted. We would be shamed. I must take her somewhere nice. Was my mother not worth a good gift of thanks?

Guilt. It bricked me in on all sides.

"She wanted real Chinese. She picked our place. I thought if she wanted real Chinese I'd give her the complete experience," I snapped. My mother hung up with a snort. I was a disappointment again.

Once, my mother sent me to school with a special lunch of fish cakes. They were my favourite; I was being rewarded for having good marks.

"What is that smell?" the teacher asked, wrinkling her nose.

The students laughed and held their noses. "It's Kelly's lunch."

The teacher tried to be understanding. "Come with me, Kelly. We'll wrap it up and keep it in the staffroom fridge until lunch time."

I got my lunch later and ran to the farthest corner of the playground to eat. After that, I told my mom I wanted only peanut butter sandwiches for lunch.

My half sister and I lived in two different planes of reality within one room. She was five years older and her mother was married to my father. She did not care that she was a disappointment. She cared about boys, dances, and rock stars. She planned to marry a rock star and live in a huge, red brick mansion. I felt the disappointment. My mother was only a concubine. I felt the guilt. I cared about nothing but success. I studied. I had no life. It is better anyway to have no life if you are a lesbian teen. It is easier that way.

I have read that many lesbian women have terrible teenage years with awful experiences filled with the pain of discovery and often rejection. I did not. I had nothing. I studied. I would make my father and mother proud, and then I would live the life I wanted quietly. Secrets. They are a deep sea diving suit against truth.

Joanne had been in my grade ten class. She always wore a plaid lumber shirt over a t-shirt and blue jeans. Everyone called her Jo-the-dyke. She didn't look like a dyke to me. She had wide hips and big breasts. I thought then that dykes should look like guys – flat chested and narrow hipped.

The sorority girls complained because she shared their gym change room, so she was allowed to change in the staff change room. I envied her. I did not like changing with the girls, even though I was gay. I am a very private person and I was Chinese in a White school. Once a girl asked if I was yellow down there, too. How do you answer a question like that?

Jo-the-Dyke was strong but she had no grace, and so she was not good at sports except shot put. She could beat anyone hands down in shot put, but nobody cared. Shot put was not a sport anyone cared about. No one cared about Jo, either. Jo was not good at school. She'd come late and skip class. When she was yelled at by a teacher, she would shrug.

Because we were both outcasts, sometimes she would sit with me at lunch in the cafeteria. I never sent her away because I was raised to be polite, but I never chose to sit with her. I would let her copy my math or French so I would not have to make conversation. I am not good at conversation.

She told me that she had a horse and liked to ride. I thought this strange. Girls like to ride, so dykes shouldn't. Girls like to spread their legs and feel the heat and leather against their sex. Girls ride, women fuck. I never rode. My mother believed it would damage me. Damage me how? I was never told. I never wanted to ride anyway, at least not horses.

"Kelly," Jo would say, "I'm going to be free someday. You wait and see."

Jo-the-Dyke left school in grade eleven and drove trucks. I heard she was killed in a winter pile up. When I think of her, I don't picture her as a frozen corpse waiting for a body bag; I see her smiling, free to be herself on the open road. I think she would like that I remember her that way.

I need to talk about secrets. You can't have secrets without having lies. I have heard people say that you can't have a good relationship if there isn't complete honesty. It surprises me that there are any relationships at all then. You tell me that you do have an open, honest relationship. I wonder. Reality is smoke. Perhaps you have forgotten that you cheated on that test and really didn't deserve that A. Or that you snitched cigarettes from your father's pack when no one was around. Perhaps you masturbated and said the stain on your sheets was from your dog, or played show and tell with the boy next door to see what boys had that girls didn't. Perhaps you told your parent or partner all these things but there are some things that embarrass you still or that are too personal, that you have not shared. There are some things that we can't even be truthful about to ourselves.

Smoke. We are all smoke. Try and catch us.

My cherry was ripped from my bush by my brother when I was fourteen. He was nineteen. The stain it left on the sheets was the colour of red brick. He had come to live with us six months before. My father was delighted by my brother's arrival. The rest of us were resentful most of the time and embarrassed at others. Jason did not know how to act properly. He did not offer the best pieces of food to his guest by placing them on their plate. Instead, he would reach out and snaffle the best pieces with his chopsticks and eat them noisily. He never knew to pour the tea, as is proper for the oldest son, and always had to be reminded. He spoke in a loud voice and was always bragging about his latest scheme for making money. None of them ever seemed to turn out, but somehow, it was never Jason's fault. My father kept bankrolling him.

My sister had gone to the movies with some girl friends and the adults in the family had gone to the races. I'd had my bath and was getting ready for bed when Jason opened my bedroom door without knocking.

"Get out!"

"Do not speak to me like that, bitch! You are only a girl."

"You can't come in here, Jason. It is not right." I was hot with embarrassment, but not fear. I had not yet learned fear. I wrapped my bath towel around me closely.

"You are very sexy. Men will want you. Are you a virgin?"

I was shocked. "Yes, of course! Don't talk like that, it's rude, Jason."

"I want you." He came in and closed my bedroom door.

"You're my half brother."

He laughed. "No, I'm not. Your father paid the Green Dragon to kidnap a boy child for him. I was only ten, but I can remember a stranger offering me money to go with him. I cried for my mother for a long time."

"My father wouldn't do anything so horrible," I protested, but I wasn't sure. My father had wanted a son so badly.

"Horrible? I am much better off than I would have been had I not been kidnapped from my mother. But, I am not your brother. I'm the man who is going to take you."

When it was over, I knew fear. Fear is a red brick stain on your life. I cried. Then I limped into the kitchen and got the fish boning knife. Jason was asleep on the couch in front of the TV. I stuck the point against his balls. He woke with a scream like a frightened girl and looked like he would be sick.

"If you ever touch me again, I will wait until you are asleep, and I'll cut your balls off."

I never told anyone what he had done. I was too ashamed, and I was sure he would lie and I would be blamed. He was the male child and perfect; I was the female child and a disappointment. My mother and Aunt Quin wondered what had happened to the knife. It was under my mattress. It is still under my mattress. Whenever the knife was mentioned, I would look at Jason and see him sweat. He never touched me again. Yet he had taken and kept something of mine, and I hated him for it.

On Saturday night, I waited outside our red brick take-out for Officer Anderson. She arrived on a bicycle. I was glad to see that she was not in uniform. Instead, she wore blue jeans and a white t-shirt. The round blue patch on her left shoulder read *Peel Police Department: Sharpshooter*. She was tougher than she looked. I wore blue jeans, too, but my tailored shirt had no badge of merit. I hoped she would like eating in a take-out kitchen.

"Hi, Kelly. Am I late?"

"No, Of...err"

"Jane." She smiled.

I smiled. "No, Jane. I thought I'd better wait outside so you'd find the place okay. Do you really want the whole Chinese experience?" There was the Steak House down the street if she had changed her mind. My mother would approve if I took her to the Steak House.

"How often does one get the chance for a genuine Chinese meal and not an American-Chinese meal?" she asked, a teasing note in her voice.

Never. "Then come in and I will cook for you."

"You, Counsellor?"

"Me. I grew up in this kitchen, and I learned to cook well before I was out of elementary school. I'm good. You are in for the whole cultural experience."

She laughed. It was a nice laugh.

The kitchen was hot and steamy. It smelt of vegetables, herbs, and the starch of rice. I showed Jane to the rough table in the back corner where I had studied and eaten most of my life. On the way, I introduced her to my family. Not my immediate family, they no longer worked in the kitchen, but to my cousins and uncles who have replaced them over the years. Canada gives preference to family members who wish to immigrate. I taught her how to greet them in Cantonese. She did not say it right and my relatives laugh at the strange sound, but they are pleased that she has tried and welcome her warmly. Most were new to Canada and they had not learned to be Canadian. If they could have read her t-shirt logo, they would have been more cautious. They thought about police as they had in the old country.

I tried to explain to Jane that Chinese languages, like First Nation languages, are tonal. The meaning for the word is changed by the lilt of the voice, so the Chinese language sounds sing-song to the Western ear. I smiled and explained that the various tones make the Chinese language hard to learn at first. She smiled in return and took the seat I offered her.

The topic reminded me of when I was a child and the children in the playground would pull up the corner of their eyes and make funny sing-song noises from behind buck teeth. They called me Charlie Chan. Children are not cruel; parents are cruel for teaching their children to be racist bigots. The taunts often hurt. You have to learn to ignore the ignorant. My mother would tell me to put up a wall between their taunts and my feelings. I imagined a red brick wall. Was the Great Wall of China made of red brick?

"They are not cultured like the Chinese. They do not know any better," my mother would say. In traditional Chinese languages, there is no word for foreigner. The word barbarian was used. Every culture has its bigotry.

I started from scratch, boning and scaling the fish with quick, sure movements. I was good with a knife. Then I chopped the vegetables and prepared them in a heated wok. Jane didn't talk. She watched my preparations with interested eyes. When it was time to eat, I sat beside her not across from her. I placed choice pieces on her plate with chopsticks. She didn't seem to find this unusual. Instead, she picked up the morsels and bit into them, looking me straight in the eye.

I was wet, moist fish. I wanted to be in her mouth, tasting her. Does she only ride a bike?

We said good-night on the sidewalk.

"That was an amazing meal and a really unique experience. Thank you, and thank your mother. Give her my best."

"I will. I'm glad you enjoyed your meal."

"Very much so. Well, good-night."

Ask her out! "Good-night." I watched her ride away. I was a private person. I feared I might have read too much into the evening. I would have done my mother great dishonour if I had misunderstood Jane's friendliness. *Was that the reason I hesitated?*

My first crush was a girl in high school. I was still in elementary school. We would stand at the same street corner to catch the bus for school. Sometimes, if the bus was crowded, she would sit beside me. I got off the bus before her. My dreams were full of adventures and twists of fate that brought us together in a happily-ever-after. I fantasized about our times together. It was sex without fear. I asked once if she liked to ride horses. She told me she did when she was younger. I considered that a good sign.

One day, I was sitting well behind her. On impulse, I rode past my stop, wanting to see her get off and enjoy the secret moment of watching her swaying hips and cute behind as she got off the bus. A guy was there waiting for her, and she hugged and kissed him. He had bad acne – red brick stains over his face. I wept.

I never had the social pressure to date. My father had been a scholar in China. He had worked toward joining the civil service. My father expected us to study, not date. Jason had been lucky to have been out of the country. He had been allowed to be a failure. My sister and I were expected to study. I did. My sister learned how to scale red brick walls at night and escape to her world of friends. My sister is not handsome and tall, she is petite and cute and very popular. My world was within; hers was wide spread.

Sarah said there was an imaginary wall down the center of our room that could not be crossed. I was in trouble if I did so. Her clutter sometimes leaked over to my side. My side was neat, orderly, and dull. Hers was a garage sale of teenage paraphernalia. So was my sister's life. During the day, she was always bouncy and smiling. She filled a room with energy and happiness. At night, she sometimes cried. I would ask the darkness if she was all right, if there was anything I could do, but the muffled reply was that she was overly tired and not to worry.

Secrets. They reveal themselves at night, but they do not resolve.

The wall between my sister and me had many different types of bricks. She was five years older – a generation of thought away from me. She was outgoing; I, introverted. My love was learning and hers was playing. I saw order; she saw a kaleidoscope of possibilities. We were not close, but we were bonded by the genes of our father.

In high school, I was greeted by "You're Sarah Li's sister?" It was not possible to live up to my sister's reputation. I was glad of that. I didn't have the energy or the smiles. I remained isolated.

I was the class Browner from whom the others came to copy homework. That all changed in grade ten when the gym teacher pulled me aside and insisted I try out for the basketball team. I am tall and strong, as I have said, and by then had gotten over the awkward years when limbs were too long and kept knocking over things. I took up basketball with the same intensity that I did everything else in my life. Perhaps my parents would not see me as a disappointment if I was a sports star.

I scored on the court and in the change room. I had matured and seeded, spreading out roots and twining others close. I was a weed of an adolescent – strong, needy, and demanding. But I was also very much a wall flower. I spread, but clung to a wall of normality. There was no coming out for me. Now I moved like a Time Lord through three worlds: Chinese, Canadian, and Alternative. In each, I was a different person. Each jump to hyper-space tore at my soul. Who was I?

Katherine Ustinov was a team forward, and forward. She played one on one with me for three years. She also played with others. Kate had a lot of team spirit. She'd had a tough life, even at that early age. Her father was abusive and her mother a closet drunk. At sixteen, when she told them she was a lesbian, they had kicked her out of the house. Her father had beaten her up first, though, and her mother had drunk and watched it happen. Kate said it was worth it. She now got welfare support and had her own apartment. Her apartment was where we all hung out: the queers, and the straights who were proud of being liberal thinkers. Kate collected conquests. I was her Chinese conquest. As the village of Cooksville was swallowed up into the urban sprawl of the city of Mississauga, Kate had great opportunities to sleep with every nation of the world.

Kate liked to be on top, so did I. The sex was good, but the dominance battle was the usual lesbian problem. Kate was noisy in bed; I was quiet. "Let's pretend," she would say, and go off into a great fantasy. Kate was always fantasizing. She had a hard time staying in reality. Reality for Kate was no fun. She went to school to play basketball, and for no other reason. Once she threw my history text across the room in disgust.

"Why are you always reading that crap?"

"To learn."

"Bullshit. By now I know everything there is to know."

I laughed. Kate got through school copying my homework and using the cheat sheets I made for her for tests and exams. "Sure you do."

Kate's eyes narrowed. "Test me. Pick a subject."

"History."

"We go through ages. In each, we learn to kill better. Then we go to war and regret it. End of story."

"Geography."

"We go through ages. In each, we learn to deplete resources quicker and pollute more thoroughly. We do so and regret it. End of story."

"Language."

"We go through ages. In each, we communicate in a different language. The message is always the same and we regret it. End of story."

"Mathematics."

"We go through ages. In each, we learn to calculate better. We have done so and now we have enough nuclear bombs to destroy the world twenty-seven times over. We regret it. End of story."

"Art?"

"We go through stages. We regret it, and that regret weeps in our art."

I laughed. Kate had cynicism down to a fine art. "So, what is our next stage?"

Kate shrugged. "Who knows? But we'll live to regret it."

Kate had a favourite fantasy. It was about making love on the court after a big game. She had a basketball net screwed to the back of the apartment building wall. It was above the handicap parking spot. No one in the building was handicapped, so the spot wasn't used much except by the occasional visitor. We'd play in the late afternoon on hot pavement. The oven-hot brick wall radiated heat over us and echoed our voices back to us like a crowd. Hot and sweaty after the game, we'd head up to her apartment. We'd barely be inside the door before Kate would be pulling the clothes off me to make love.

For her birthday, I made a tape of a play-off college game. If she could wait long enough, I'd turn it on and then she'd really get hot. We'd go at it until we were exhausted, then we'd shower and I'd have to go home. There would be someone else there at night. Kate hated to be alone. Going down in the elevator, I'd feel myself cross over into my Chinese self. It tore at my soul every time.

I remember the first time I stayed over, Kate watched me slip the boning knife under my pillow.

"What is *that* for? I'm not into S&M."

"You're safe. It is to protect me from spirits."

"You believe in ghosts?"

"Many Chinese do. The belief in the spirits of our ancestors is very strong."

"You have an ancestor who wants to see you dead?"

"No, my fear is the ghost of Christmas Past," I joked cynically. "The knife wards off nightmares."

"You want to talk about it?"

"No."

When it came time to consider a university, my father told me that there would not be much money. At that time, I did not know my father was rich. He had led us all to believe that his money was all tied up in loans and the business. He told me I could stay at home, and he would pay for my food, but there would be little money for tuition, books, or living expenses.

Around the same time, my brother Jason was arrested on an arson charge. It appeared that criminal life was what suited Jason best. Unfortunately, he was not good at that, either. My father hired him an expensive lawyer and so there was little available cash for my education. It was unthinkable that my father would liquidate any of his investments to help me out.

"I hate him," my sister said of Jason. "I fucking hate him! Don't you?"

"Yes."

"I swear I'm going to kill him."

"Why?"

"He shamed me."

The question was on my lips, but I swallowed it. To ask her if the shame was rape would be to reveal my own shame. I remained silent. Would things have been different if I had not? I don't know. I was silent. So many are. We women bind our secrets to our souls with lies.

A scholarship finally made my future possible. I got a job as a cook in a Chinese restaurant downtown, found a cheap apartment, and enrolled at Toronto University. I studied law. I always wanted to be a lawyer. I was going to be a great lawyer and put people like Jason behind bars for good.

My sister got pregnant when I was in grade nine and she was in her first year of college. The father was a Chinese boy from Hong Kong. They were married in a hall in North York. Once the Chinese community was downtown, but the City built a new town hall in Nathan Phillips Square, and the city councillors did not like the scruffy shops of the Chinese being just around the corner. The dead chickens hanging by their legs in the window, the barrels of hundred year old eggs in their clit glubs, the Buddhist Temple – every smell, sight, and sound offended City Hall, even though the Chinese community paid their taxes and encouraged their children to learn to fit into Western society. They were slowly forced out and moved to North York. North York is now Ontario's Chinatown.

As far as I know, my sister's marriage is a happy one. They have three children, all boys. This did not please my father; it was not his name that would be passed on. My sister's husband took accounting and worked for a Chinese import business in North York. My sister learned bookkeeping and worked for a local hardware store. They have a home in a subdivision in Mississauga, close to Burnhamthorpe and Dixie. My sister is a good mother. She adores her twin boys, but she fights a lot with her oldest son. He looks like Jason. Secrets.

I do not plan on being a mother, but I try to be a good aunt. I visit my nephews regularly and take them places. They are young but seem to have good minds, and their parents have taught them to be polite and self disciplined. My sister has set the same standards for her children that she rebelled against as a child. All things come full circle. Sarah's oldest child is named John. Not Jonathan, just John.

John and I talked about his name once.

"I am named after a toilet."

"Nonsense," I said.

"Mom is stricter with me than my brothers."

"You are the oldest."

He nodded. "Mom said she worked very hard in school and got excellent marks, and I must do the same. She only quit school to have me."

I smiled. Secrets bonded to lies become the breeding ground for myths.

Some weeks after my dinner with Jane Anderson, she contacted me. I had not had the nerve to phone her again although I had thought about it often.

"I was wondering if you are doing anything Saturday," she asked.

"Nothing special."

"I was wondering if you would be free to come to a Maple Leaf hockey game at the Air Canada Centre. I was given some tickets. Chrissy is going to spend the day with her grandparents."

"Chrissy?"

"My daughter. She's three. Can you come?"

"Sure. I like hockey." I was afraid to say anything else. She might hear the surprise and disappointment, although I would try to hide it well. I didn't know she was married.

"Great! If you give me your address, I'll pick you up about noon."

I do so, too surprised to think very clearly.

Jane's daughter is called Christine, named after her father Christopher. Her father was a cop too. He was killed when he was hit by a car as he directed traffic around the scene of an accident. The driver was drunk. Christine had not been born then, so she never knew her father. I learn all this as we drive along the Gardener Expressway.

"I am sorry. It must be hard to raise a daughter by yourself."

"It is very difficult with the shift work, but my parents and my in-laws are wonderful. Chrissy is so used to being with them that they are like second homes for her."

We have great seats. They are season tickets that the Anderson's have. Now and again, they give the tickets to Jane.

"You are confused." Jane smiled.

I'm startled. Could she read minds? "Yes. I guess. I'm not sure why you invited me."

"Because I want to get to know you better."

I don't know how to take that. The hard part of being a closet gay is that you don't have any way of easily establishing a relationship with another person. You are operating in the darkness of lies and secrets.

Jane looks at me. "I need you to know that I'm gay. It's not just a friendship I'm looking for, and I got the feeling last month when you made dinner for me that there was a possibility that you might feel the same way. Am I wrong?"

"No. You are not wrong." The words were out of my mouth before I could consider them. Jane kept me totally off balance. I try to get a handle on what is going on. "You were married. You have a child."

"Many gay women do."

"What happened in the last three years to make you want an alternative life style?"

"Nothing. I knew I was gay before I married Chris. Chris and I met at the Police College. We really hit it off and became good friends. One thing led to another and I thought, why not? I was getting a lot of pressure from home to marry and have a family. I didn't think I could ever bring myself to come out, and I liked Chris. I guess that sounds pretty cowardly and shallow, but I did my best to make the marriage work. I think we were happy enough. Maybe there were no bells and whistles, but there was a lot of fun and contentment."

"Did Chris know you were gay?"

"Yes, of course. I wouldn't deceive him. It wouldn't be fair. He said he didn't care, as long as I felt I could be happy with him and didn't stray."

She looked at her hands for a bit, weighing her actions. "I was really angry and shocked when Chris was killed, but a part of me was relieved, too, that I was no longer married to him. I had fulfilled my societal obligations and I was free again. That's awful, isn't it?" She looked up, eyes filled with tears.

I'm not good at this sort of stuff. I try, but the words come out blunt. "It wasn't right. Then again, how many of us do the right things? Society, culture, belief, they all push us into roles that we don't particularly want to play. Perhaps that is why so many of us are depressed. You didn't wish Chris dead. He died. Bad things happen. You can't hold on to that guilt and make it your own. I don't believe that any of us have truly honest relationships with anyone. All we can do is come as close as we can and try to work through issues as they arise."

"Maybe." She looks out onto the field with blank eyes. "It's just that living a lie seems so unfair to Chris."

I consider this. "Perhaps. But from what you said, he was happy with the relationship. That's more than most people find in marriage, and because of you, there is a part of Chris that lives on in his daughter. When you put it all on a scale, it seems to me to balance, and I figure that is about all you can hope for in this world."

"You are rationalizing."

I laughed. "Of course. I'm a lawyer." Then I got serious again. "I can't make it better for you, Jane. I wish I could. All I can tell you is that it doesn't matter to me what you have done in the past. I like you. I'd like to see you again."

She smiled. The game was good. The momentum swung back and forth, and it ended in a tie. That's all you can hope for in life. It is all smoke anyway.

We had dinner at an Italian restaurant. Pizza. She teased me about my love for Italian food. I told her that noodles were invented in China and so spaghetti was really Chinese. She drove me home and I invited her up for a drink. It was safe to do so. I had left my mom at Aunt Quin's for the night.

"Sorry, I can't. I have to go say good-night to Chrissy. I'm on the graveyard shift tonight. Another time. Please?" Her eyes seemed earnest, almost frightened.

I leaned over and kissed her lips gently. "I'll be in touch."

I went up to my condo, and, too restless to settle, I cleaned the place and did the laundry. Then, too tired to carry on, I snagged a beer from the fridge and flopped down in an easy chair with my feet up. I didn't drink very often, but that night just called for a beer. I wondered what was going on between Jane and me.

I'd had relationships before, a few very serious ones. I knew the heady excitement of newfound love and the heat of discovery. My reactions to Jane, however, had been totally different. I found myself not in control. Instead, it felt like I was free falling and had no idea which way was up anymore. Jane was like no one I had ever met. She didn't play mind games; she just told you straight up where she stood and left the ball in your court. I felt way out of my league. Jane was playing hard ball with my emotions. I mused over the day for some time until the second beer was gone and I fell asleep.

The phone ringing woke me up.

With a start, I fought my way back to consciousness and I hauled myself up to pick up.

The voice was frantic. "Kelly? Kelly!"

"Sarah? What's the matter?"

"Oh God, Kelly."

I felt my heart tightening. "Sarah, what's happened?"

"I've killed him."

"Who?"

"I've killed Jason."

"Where are you?"

"At home."

"Have you phoned anyone else or talked to anyone else?"

"No."

"Don't. Are Hu and the boys there?"

"No. He's taken the boys camping with the Scouts for the weekend."

"Anyone else there?"

"J...just Jason."

"Sit down right where you are. Don't touch anything. Don't move. Don't answer the door or the phone until I get there. Understood?"

"Yes."

I put down the phone and gripped the edge of the table. My heart was drumming like a sledgehammer. *What was I going to do now? The Golden Mountain shakes.*

Her Story

White bread and mayonnaise – that had been my life. My father is an accountant and my mother an elementary school teacher. Middle management, middle class, middle of the road – that was my family. My brother was born first. He was born in the spring, as my parents planned, and named Carl after his grandfather. My parents thought it a good, sensible name. I was born in the spring two years later, as planned. I was christened Jane – a plain, sensible name.

Our house was halfway down the road in a subdivision where each of the roads was named after a famous ship or naval battle. We lived on Midway. Our house was neither big nor small. There were three bedrooms, two baths, a dog and cat and a fenced-in backyard. When I was young, we had a second-hand car, a plastic wading pool, and a swing set in the backyard. I remember little, but have seen it many times on the eight millimetre film my father took with the Brownie movie camera that my mother got him for Christmas one year. The film is badly faded and jumps a good deal. It always ends with a series of white dots. Our early life was framed by Kodak and saved on reels at the back of a closet. I'm still in the closet.

As we got older, the family got a new car and my mom got to drive the used vehicle. The swing set was replaced with a barbecue, and the wading pool with a small in ground pool. I was still in the closet, but I had been known, from time to time, to share the closet with others. I also married and had a daughter. This comes later in my story.

Growing up, our family went to church on Sundays. We were Anglicans – a Catholic service with Protestant ideals, middle of the road religion. After church, we visited our grandparents. My mother's one Sunday, my father's the next. At my mother's parents, we had turkey and stuffing for dinner. At my father's parents, we had lamb and roast potatoes. In the summer, we didn't bother going to church. My mother said we enjoyed God's sunlight instead. My father went golfing and prayed for a good round. In our house, we respected God but didn't fear Him. God brought Shrove Tuesday pancakes, Christmas, and chocolate Easter bunnies, so He was all right with Carl and me.

My brother and I did well in school. We were not the top of the class, but we were not near the bottom, either. I excelled at sports. Carl became an accountant; I became a police officer.

I suppose since I had a perfectly normal life, with good parents and love and security, I should have become a teacher, nurse, or secretary and married the boy next door. Instead, I discovered I was gay and became a cop because I liked wearing the uniform and driving with flashing lights and sirens. Perhaps if I had gone to church during the summers, I would have been "normal" like everyone else in my family. Personally, it didn't bother me much. I stayed in the closet because of my family. Their way was the middle way; mine was a dance to a different drummer.

We all dance. We all dance to the pressures of family, society, faith, an endless mound of expectations. We all have our lone dances, as well. Those solo performances that we indulge in when no one is looking. Some of us only hear the beat of that drummer far off and on rare occasions. Others of us are driven crazy by the rhythm of the beat. We are drawn from our list of expectations; the Pied Piper of our souls leading us down strange, exciting paths. The cost, if caught, is rejection and scorn. I listened to the drummer and became an explorer in alternative worlds, but I remained a secret explorer for many years. I would sneak from my white bread and mayonnaise world and teleport into gay bars and a woman's bed. It was a liberating but exhausting experience. Each trip ripped at my soul.

I remember being quite little and wearing a pretty dress to school. My teacher said I was so cute. I realized this was a good thing, but I wasn't sure why. I found my dress very restrictive. My mother had warned me not to show my underpants, but to sit like a little lady. I sat in the sandbox and played with a plastic bulldozer. I carefully kept my legs together and wished I was in shorts. Why would I want to be cute when I could be free?

I recall sitting in the back seat of our 1956 Ford. It was green and my father was very proud of it. He called it a status symbol. My mother was driving, and beside her sat my aunt.

"I was shocked. I didn't think Barb was like that. I've known her family for years."

"She and Bill have gone steady since ninth grade."

"Yes, but she should have waited until they were married this spring. How far along is she?"

"Five months, Sally said."

"She'll be showing soon. There will be some nasty talk."

"She's going to go stay with her aunt in Calgary until after the birth."

"That's for the best."

I listened and wondered. "Why is Sally bad, mom?"

Silence from the front seat. In the 50s, adults thought children were deaf to adult conversations. "She is not bad; she just did a bad thing."

"What?"

"She is going to have a baby and she is not married."

I think about this. "But Sally and Bill are in love. You said when people are in love they make a baby. Why is that wrong?"

"You'll understand when you are older."

I am older and I still do not understand. How can love be wrong, no matter what form it takes?

I went to a small country school. At recess, in the cold weather we played hockey and in the warm weather we played baseball. A dirt path worn into the shape of a diamond was where we played. There were no bases, there was no need – we all knew in our minds where the base should be. Foul balls were a problem. Foul to the left, and the ball arched over the hedge and into the grumpy neighbour's rose garden. Foul to the right, and the ball dropped over the fence into the pioneer graveyard. I was not like the other girls who squealed in dismay and ran to get the duty teacher. I just opened the gate and walked around the dead to get the ball. If it was in the neighbour's garden, I peeked around the hedge to see that the coast was clear and then ran as fast as I could to retrieve the ball. All the girls played on one side of the school and all the boys on the other. I was never sure why, until Brenda explained to me that boys had cooties and they could give them to us.

I wondered why it was okay to walk home with them and play with them on weekends and in the summer. Brenda explained it was only at school that we were in danger. I suspected I already had cooties, whatever that was, because I'd have preferred to be playing with the boys.

As I got older, I became very envious of my brother. He could pee standing up and had no problem learning to spit. He was allowed to wear comfortable clothes except on Sunday, when he had to wear a tie. Still, I figured a tie was better than a garter belt and nylons. By the time I got into them and my training bra, I felt like a work horse all harnessed up. The concept, when you think about it, is much the same. Riding is riding. Perhaps that is why men find garter belts sexy.

Then I had my first period. I thought I was dying. My embarrassed mother explained that this would happen every month for most of my life because I could have a baby now. Now I was really jealous of my brother. He didn't have periods. He didn't have cramps. He got to make babies and walk away; I got to blow up like a balloon. It was around this time that I realized that God had to be male.

For some reason, the other girls seemed to be all excited about nylons, periods, and bras. They seemed to think it was all wonderful. I started to think that I should have been a boy. Probably, God forgot to put the extra parts on or something. My mom seemed horrified when I suggested this.

"Jane! It's a terrible sin to want to be the other sex."

"Why?" I wondered. It seems it was because a couple of old guys living thousands of years ago in the Middle East with little or no education said so. It was in the Bible, and so it was truth.

I considered this information. "How do we know they were right?"

"The prophets were inspired by God."

It sounded like some sort of biblical clubhouse to me. A sign that stupid boys put up saying "no girls allowed".

I felt guilty for thinking I might be a boy. I hadn't meant to sin, and I was hoping God would forgive me and not send me to Hell for thinking His rules were sexist. I decided what I was really was a tomboy. It's okay to be this, because tomboys grow up to be normal and not sinful. Growing up is complicated.

Years later, I met Kelly Li in court. She was defending a guy who was associated with a smuggling ring that handled everything from fake designer watches from China to drugs from Afghanistan. He was only lower management, but he was my first big arrest and I wanted to make it stick. Kelly came on really strong, and by the end of the case, seeded enough doubt to get the guy about half the time he deserved. She was a woman I could get to hate. I was sure hoping I did not meet her in court very often. She got under my skin big time.

I think what I hated about her most was that I noticed her right away. She stood out in a crowd. Everyone seemed like smoke around her and she, the hot, roaring flame. I couldn't take my eyes off her. Her eyes barely met mine. I was not a woman; I was Officer Anderson. She had kept me on the stand until the sweat was trickling down my back, until I was starting to second guess myself. *Did I follow all the correct procedures? Damn it, yes I did.* I might have been a rookie then, but I knew my job. She was not able to find fault, but she sure tried.

I am used to others finding fault. Fault was how my mother demonstrated her love.

"Jane, do straighten your shoulders. Don't slouch around like a guy."

"Why do guys get to slouch?"

"We are not built the same, Jane. Shoulders back, straighten your neck. Best impression first, as your grandmother would say."

What she meant by this was that a woman was to enter a room with a poised look and breasts thrusting. I tried, but I never developed enough to thrust with any conviction. Besides, I felt stupid. Brenda told me that you had to have good knockers to wear a bikini. You had to have the Monroe build – 35, 22, 35. The two of us tried. I underachieved at 32, 20, 30. Brenda overachieved at 38, 30, 38. Neither of us was going to sing Happy Birthday to any presidents or stop our men from getting the seven year itch.

My first kiss from a guy was when I was eight. He was the son of a farmhand, and we were in grade two together. He had made a fort in the woods from a fallen pine tree. Together we crawled under the fragrant bush and he kissed me. No bells and whistles. It was a great fort, though, and I made a note to take Brenda there to play.

I never questioned that I would grow up and marry and have kids. That was what women do. Even during the sexual revolution of the sixties and the women's liberation movement, I didn't sway from this belief. I just modified it. I would grow up, have a career, marry a liberal minded guy, and have babies.

I think I was into my high school years before it sunk in with me that some women didn't marry guys. That some women liked women. I was shocked. Some of these women were famous. They were women I respected. How could you respect someone who was sinful? I started to question. God was dead, the radical fringe of my generation said. He appeared to be dead, or at least high on magic mushrooms and not paying attention. Had He not noticed the Cold War? Viet Nam? The Cuban Missile Crisis? The Berlin Wall? Did He not care that women did not own their own bodies or that men controlled everything? I gave up on God. It was the easiest way to give up the root of the guilt. Now I didn't have to mind that my parents hated gays. They had been brainwashed by the Church and didn't know any better. But what about me? I knew what I *didn't* believe, but what *did* I believe?

I was a second generation hippie, as most of my generation were. They had buried the movement, complete with coffin, on Haight-Ashbury before I took up long hair, love beads, and bell-bottoms. I watched Woodstock on TV, second hand, and saw the Beatles in concert, not at the Cavern. The Rolling Stones had gathered some moss by the time I embraced them, and Viet Nam had ceased to be a police action and was a war of a thousand ugly days.

I continued to go to school, but my weekends were hazy from grass and lava lamps. I liberated my mind by following everyone else. We were cookie-cutter freedom seekers dancing, dancing, dancing, but never individually.

My first dance was the senior prom. I went with Ralf Parks. He seemed nice enough. He played on the senior football team and so was considered quite a catch. I was still a junior. I wore a pink silk gown and pearls. My mother and grandmothers said I looked beautiful. I felt like I was wrapped up in butcher paper. I would have preferred to wear the tux; it looked cool. I take it Ralf didn't think much of the dress, because he spent most of the evening in the back seat of his Volkswagen Bug trying to get me out of it. Finally, I kicked him where it hurts, no easy matter when wearing a formal inside a tin can, and used the taxi fare my mother gave me to get home.

My father wanted to punch out Ralf's lights. I told him that wasn't necessary; I'd already damaged the light of his life. My father paled, but managed a laugh.

"Did you learn anything from this experience, Jane?" my mother asked.

I assumed the answer was supposed to be that men only want one thing and women are to withhold it until they are offered marriage. That was not what I learned. "Yes," I answered promptly. I m going to be a police officer. There was a woman cop at the dance, and she kept Ralf by his car for a talk while I phoned for a cab. That's what I want to be – a uniformed cop with a gun."

Now it was time for my mother to pale. I'm sure she prayed each night that I would get over this stage, just like I got over being a hippie.

Christmas at our house was a happy ritual that had very little to do with God. We did manage to squeeze in a visit to church on Christmas morning, but it was an effort. My brother and I would wake up early and tuck into the stockings that Santa had left us. There would be nylons, jewellery, make-up, games, a few coins, and some candy and fruit for me each year. Carl always did better. He'd get action figures, Match Box cars, and neat things like a jackknife or compass.

Then we'd have breakfast and rush to get ready for church. Joy to the world: God gave us a son by taking a virgin without her permission. I guess the Church provided God with sanctuary, because anywhere else, He'd have been arrested. As I got older, I would toy with the idea that Christ was a cross-dresser. His/Her philosophy of love seemed far more feminine than male. Maybe Mary was a dominant mother. I tried to imagine an unmarried Jewish man of thirty, walking around the Middle East two thousand years ago, attracting guys to travel with him and form a new church based on love. It's a stretch without bringing up subjects that are a sin according to the Old Testament. My sacrilegious humour was not warmly received in my white bread and mayonnaise world. My mother would blush and murmur that I was going through a rebellious age.

After church, we'd head home and open our family presents.

My father would hand out the gifts and we'd all have to wait until everyone had theirs before we could open anything. Then there was a good deal of rending and tearing, laughing, hugs, and kisses of thanks. The grandparents would arrive later, and the whole process would start again. Dinner made an Army mess look like child's play. Aunts, uncles, and cousins were added to the family mix during the day, and the feast was an amazing sight. We kids had our own table, where we had to watch our manners and not disturb the adults too much.

I mention Christmas because when I was twelve, my unmarried aunt from out west came to visit. "Your Aunt Edith from out west" was a legend in the family. She didn't fit into the white bread and mayonnaise mould. She owned a horse and rode, lived on a farm, and worked as a nurse with Indian children. Another female nurse lived with her and was taking care of the horses, dogs and cats while she was visiting us. I grew up thinking that "out west" was vaguely socially unacceptable but an exciting place to be.

My Aunt Edith did not disappoint. On Christmas day, Carl and I got Daisy BB rifles and real Indian drums. They are, even to date, the best gifts I have ever received. I remember looking up at my Aunt Edith with stars in my eyes and her smiling back with a gentle, knowing smile. She died of cancer a year later and left everything to her friend. I wish I had known her as well as she knew me. I still have the rifle and drum. They stayed in the closet with me for many years.

Aunt Edith, Carl, and I had lots of fun together. She took us on adventures every day. Sometimes they were just walks in the neighbourhood, and other times we'd hop a bus or train and end up at the zoo or the Science Centre. Whatever we did, Aunt Edith made us see it with different eyes.

She could walk through the local park and spy the mottled brown of a hawk high in a nook of a tree or point out the beauty of the pastel shades of a gum tree bark. We'd sing silly songs at the top of our lungs and not care what others thought, or we'd have a snowball fight while waiting for a bus. After the New Year, it was time for her to leave.

"I'll miss you so much."

"I'll miss you too." Aunt Edith smiled and stopped packing to give me a hug.

"Will you come back soon?"

"I don't think I'll be back to the east again, Jane. But maybe someday you can come to Vancouver Island and meet my friend Cleo. I think the two of you will get on very well."

"I'd love that."

Aunt Edith zipped up her travelling case and sat on the bed and I sat beside her. "I want you to remember this, Jane. What is right is what feels good in both your heart and soul. Never let anyone dictate to you what is right or wrong."

I never saw my Aunt Edith again. When I got older, I went out west to Vancouver Island as often as I could and stayed on the old homestead with Cleo and her new partner Tracy. I thought the world of both of them, and they called me their adopted daughter. Cleo and I always took a visit to my Aunt Edith's grave while I was there. Cleo took good care of it and held the memory of Edith close to her heart.

"There are many kinds of love, Jane. What Edith and I shared was very special, and I will never get over losing her so young. What Tracy and I have is a special sort of love too, but different. No one can take over the part of my heart that belongs to your Aunt Edith, and no one can take over the part of my heart that belongs to my Tracy."

I understood, and so would Aunt Edith. She'd be happy for them.

I lost my virginity in my first year of university. "Lost" isn't actually the correct word. I gave away my virginity. I was tired of being the only virgin I knew. Brad was a really sweet guy, tender and caring. Smug, of course, guys can't keep themselves from being smug when they score, especially if it is a virgin. Guys are very basic life forms. Anyway, I gave it away on a second-hand mattress on the floor of an attic apartment. No bells or whistles. I guess I should have had one of those pretend orgasms that we women are so famous for, and thanked Brad profusely for being so manly in deflowering me. Instead, I put on my clothes and went home. We continued to sleep together for the next couple of years, and there never were any bells and whistles, although it did give me some sexual relief. I acted like a real bitch. I'm sure the poor guy is still in therapy.

I also discovered my orientation while at university doing a degree in criminology. I met Victoria Barbarelli. She had legs that went all the way to tomorrow and was a long distance runner. We met at a bar, but not socially. I was working tables and she was the manager. Vic kept a poison ivy plant in a pot behind the bar. Anyone caused her girls any grief and the next glass of beer was on the house. She'd rub the lip of the glass against the plant and then saunter over with a fresh drink for the troublemaker.

"Hey, Big Boy, I gotta ask you to keep your hands to yourself and watch your language around my girls, okay? Here's a little something on the house to remember us by." The fucker went home happy and woke up in the morning with the itch. To us girls, Vic was a hero.

There was a story about some guy not taking Vic's advice seriously. As Vic turned to leave, he reached out and pinched her backside. The next second, his chair went over backwards and somehow, in the confusion, the chair leg got rammed into his family jewels. Vic apologized profusely and explained that he had knocked himself off balance reaching for something and the chair landed on his dignity. She helped him to the door and told him not to come back, because people would probably laugh. She walked back into a silent bar and smiled.

"That's what happened, wasn't it folks?" No one disagreed. Vic didn't very often have trouble in her bar.

I became her lover in my third year. There had been a lot of sexual undertones in our conversations, but nothing had come of it. I was just finishing my shift and Brad had come to pick me up. Vic sauntered over and put her arm around me. "Sorry, Brad, Jane's going home with me tonight. Aren't you, Jane?"

The two of them looked at me – Brad with hurt angry eyes, and Vic with burning desire. "I'll call you," I said to Brad.

"Don't bother." He turned on his heel and was gone. Can't say I blamed him.

Vic leaned close and nuzzled my neck. "Ever made it with a woman before?"

"No."

"Scared?"

"Yes."

"Want to change your mind?"

"No."

"Its going to be good, babe." And it was. It was all bells and whistles. It was wild and hot and good. We had two years together, but I knew we were on borrowed time. Vic didn't make commitments, especially to a woman who wanted to be a cop.

"We don't need cops in my world, babe," she would explain. "In my perfect world, everyone plays by the rules or I get even. It's a better way. Fast and guaranteed."

"You have to let the law handle these things," I argued.

"Babe, in my world, I am the law." That was true. Vic was a law unto herself.

I had taken Brad home to meet my parents and they had liked him very much. They were really disappointed when we broke up. The parental guilt trip was made worse by the secret knowledge that I'd treated Brad badly and dumped him for a wild woman. I never took Vic home to meet my parents. There was no point. She wouldn't have gone, and if she had, it would have only been to give my parents heart attacks. Vic had a poison ivy vine tattoo that started at her ankle on her left side and wound its way all the way to the back of her ear. She wasn't white bread and mayonnaise material; she was more crack pipes and reefer material.

The second time that I met Kelly Li was on a cliff face near

Hamilton. My girlfriend had joined a rock climbing club and she
had taken me along as a guest. I was halfway up the cliff face when
I realized that the sexy ass above me belonged to the lawyer from
Hell. I'm not by nature vengeful or quick tempered, but that woman
had got under my skin big time, and I acted before I thought. I
scrambled up and cut her off, leaving her clinging to the face with
nowhere to go. It was petty and childish, and I enjoyed it
immensely.

She was up the cliff after me as soon as she regained her balance, and tried to use her extra height to intimidate me. As if. Kelly
was only about an inch taller and I'd had Vic as a partner, who not
only towered over me but was rumoured to eat her meat raw. I'll
admit I never actually saw Vic do this, but I wouldn't have put anything past her. Kelly and I exchanged barbs and before it came to
fisticuffs, I rappelled down to my girlfriend.

"Who's who?"

"A lawyer," I said as I worked to unbuckle my harness.

"Where do you know her from?"

Jealousy there.

"Court. She's the lawyer from Hell I told you about."

"You didn't tell me she was so good looking."

"Don't be fooled by the exterior goods. If you went to bed with
that one, you'd probably wake up alone with your liver missing."

"She sells body parts?"

"No, I suspect she eats them. She sure went for my blood in
court."

Looking back, I am not sure why I was so offended by my day in
court with Kelly Li. I think there is a myth, at least in the white
bread and mayonnaise world, that the sort of people who go into
police work do so because they respect the law and want to make the
world a better place. No. In fact, the psychological profile of the
average cop is almost identical to that of a lifetime criminal. They
both have trouble with regimented lifestyles, they like excitement,
they tend to think on their feet, and they are lone wolves. For me it
was the uniform and sirens and getting to ride around in a squad
filled with all this heavy duty commando equipment that won me
over. So I really should have admired Kelly's ability to make the
best of an impossible situation. My irritation might have been irra-
tional, but the strength of the emotional reaction was not.

I'm ahead of myself again. After I graduated from university, I
never saw Vic again. She didn't come to my graduation, but we had
some good sex afterwards. Then she helped me pack my car, kissed
me gently, and smiled good-bye. That was it. We never talked
about breaking up. There was no agony of leaving; there was just a

kiss and a smile. I imagine Vic found a new love pretty quickly. I moped about all summer. I hated the restriction of again being the daughter in my parents' house instead of a woman with a lover. I missed the sex. I missed the independence, and I missed living on the edge with Vic. When it was time to head off to the police academy, I damn near ran to the car.

So, I met Chris Anderson at the Police Academy, when I was feeling particularly vulnerable. I missed having a partner, and I was feeling guilty because I was insisting on being a cop and not a teacher like my mom, or a nurse like my aunt had been. Hell, my parents would have even let me be an accountant like my father and brother, as long as I'd give up the idea of being a cop. I wouldn't.

I guess somewhere in my head, the guilt interfered with the logic, and I thought I could make up for Brad and Vic and a career in the police by dating Chris. It was just about then that my biological alarm clock went off and set me on a path of no return.

"This isn't going to work," I told Chris.

"Of course it is. We love each other, don't we?"

"Yes, I guess, but you know my last partner was a woman."

"So you are bisexual. Lots of people are. We are not just lovers, we are good friends. We get on well together, our families like each other, and we work in the same field. Aren't you happy with me?"

"Yes, I'm happy." Actually, "contented" would have been a better word. I was contented with Chris. There were no bells or whistles like there'd been with Vic, but then again, there wasn't the fear of police raids, either. We bought a small house in a subdivision on the edge of Cooksville and settled down contentedly. I was pregnant almost immediately. Look at me then, I was like so many women. I was living society's dream with a good man, in a nice home, a child on the way, a mortgage, and an education and retirement plan. Caught in a middle-of-the-road existence, I was content, and so terribly sad. I had not danced to my drummer but to guilt.

It is the guilt that binds women to their unhappiness. I had a beautiful white wedding. We served a mayonnaise salad before the chicken course. My father beamed, my brother talked to Chris about his responsibilities, and my mother cried. Our honeymoon was in Hawaii. Everyone was so happy when I got pregnant. My friend Brenda gave me a shower. I was living the North American dream, and I could have screamed.

Screaming. They said I did, although I don't remember. What I remember was the numbness, the stupefying numbness that made it impossible for me to get my mind around the fact that Chris was dead. How could he be dead? We'd had an early dinner together before he left for work. It was a cold, rainy night, and he wasn't looking forward to the numerous fender benders that the change in the weather would cause. I put the plastic rain hood on his cap and he slipped into his yellow rain coat before kissing me good-bye. How could Chris be dead? I was having his baby.

It was a five car pile up. Nothing serious, just bent fenders and bruised egos. There were two squads at the scene, four officers. Two were taking down statements while two directed traffic.

Allison was at one end of the pile up and Chris at the other, feeding the traffic through a single lane until the cars and debris could be cleared.

Allison said it was raining hard, but they had put out flares and had the squad lights flashing. Chris had just waved a bunch of cars through and had turned to watch while Allison took her turn. Allison saw it happen. She said it was like slow motion, although it was over in a second. She screamed to Chris to watch out, but he didn't hear her over the traffic and rain. The white car came belting past the red flares and flashing lights and hit Chris square in the back. Chris flew off into the darkness, and the car slammed on its brakes and tail-spun off the road and dug into the muddy banks on the far side of the highway.

They searched for almost an hour before they found Chris buried in some bushes forty feet away. He was dead. The autopsy said he died instantly. It was so senseless. The drunk driver got seven years for manslaughter. Manslaughter. Life slaughter. Dream slaughter. *What do I tell my daughter? Bad things happen; there is no sense.* Sometimes when I am out there on rainy nights, I can see it all happen in my mind, even though I wasn't there. I look at the reflection of the red lights smeared by rain on the road, and it is Chris's blood, Chris's life draining away. On those nights, I am a coward, clinging to the edge of the road with eyes darting back and forth, looking for danger. I do not want my daughter to be an orphan.

I was in my second trimester when Chris died. The department was very good and gave me an extended leave. Chris's insurance allowed me to pay down the mortgage so I could meet the monthly payments and not lose the house. My family was there, providing a white blanket of comfort.

The funeral was large. When a cop dies, each department sends a representative. I remember very little about it. The images all blend together except for the moment when I dropped a single rose onto the coffin from our unborn daughter. Then I cried.

It was a very bad time, made worse because inside I felt freed by the events. The guilt of that secret weighed heavily on my soul. It seemed so unfair to Chris. I never willed him dead and I mourned his loss, but a part of me rejoiced and I hated myself for that.

When my time came, my parents and Brenda went with me to the hospital. Brenda had done the prenatal classes with me and came in with me. Christine was born healthy and strong a few hours later. The people at the hospital were wonderful. Everyone knew the story; everyone cared. I cared too but not as much as I should have. The red stain of Chris's death was a heavy guilt.

It was a rainy night the next time that my path crossed Kelly's. I was called to be the back-up squad at a single car accident. The car had turned onto an entrance ramp to the expressway, lost control, and rolled down the bank. My first reaction was that the driver was most likely drunk, but when I got there, it was an older Chinese woman trapped inside and the ambulance attendants were having a hard time with her. She was confused and afraid.

I removed my hat. With my yellow slicker on, there was no indication that I was a police officer. Often, older people, especially those with a foreign background, are afraid of the police. Mostly she was babbling in Chinese, but occasionally she would use an English phrase. She wanted her daughter. I got the daughter's number from her and asked my partner to have the station phone her.

I knelt down in the mud and talked to the woman while the paramedic and fire department got on with their jobs. I talked quietly about what the people around her were doing and assured her that she was not in trouble because she'd had an accident. I couldn't smell alcohol, but the woman wasn't quite right, either. I asked the paramedics to make sure they tested for drugs at emergency. Gradually, the woman calmed down. I asked her what happened and she told me that she couldn't remember. I asked her about her daughter and her face beamed with pride.

"So what does your daughter do?"

"I'm a lawyer,"

The voice behind me was cold, and tight with stress. I turned to look and saw the lawyer from Hell. I should have known when it started to rain that it was going to be one of those nights. Kelly knelt down and took her mother's hand and started talking softly to her in Chinese. I was ignored. Our cold war was continuing. I got up, put on my hat, and sought the comfort and warmth of my squad to write up a report. I didn't want to take any chances that the lawyer from Hell would sue me on some trumped up charge. I did everything by the book and made sure my report was detailed.

So I was surprised, and worried, when a few weeks later I got a message to call Kelly Li. What was the lawyer from Hell up to now?

I phoned from the station, making it official. "This is Officer Anderson. I have a message to call this number to speak to Kelly."

"Officer Anderson, this is Kelly Li over at the Crown Attorney's Office."

"I thought you were in criminal law working for Barrs, Miller, and Wang."

"Now I work as a Crown Attorney."

"Welcome to the other side." I heard the edge to my voice and warned myself to be careful. Kelly Li could be a dangerous enemy. She ignored my remark.

"Last week my mother had a stroke and rolled her car. You were very kind to her, and she wanted me to express her thanks."

Now I was surprised. I had not considered that this call could be positive. "It was my job. How is she?"

"She had another stroke on the way to the hospital, but she seems to have recovered, although she is not as active as she has been in the past."

"I'm glad she is okay. She was scared."

"Yes, she would be."

I tried to end the conversation. My feelings were mixed. It was nice of her to phone, but I didn't trust this woman. "Thanks for calling. Please give your mother my best."

"There is something else."

This was it, I figured. My stomach tightened. "What?"

"My mother wants to give you a gift."

"Counsellor, you know better."

"Yes, but my mother doesn't. She wanted me to give you money. It is the Chinese way. I thought perhaps we could find some middle ground, and I might be able to thank you by taking you to dinner."

"With you?" I was incredulous.

"Yes."

I tried to think but my brain was having trouble getting around my bias against this woman. I'd intended to make an excuse. "All right," I said instead. *Why? I have no idea.*

I spent the rest of the week kicking myself emotionally around the block. My logic and self preservation had told me to decline, but desire had recognized the hot woman from the courtroom and short-wired my common sense. There was the single mom guilt, too. Working shift, I often have to farm Chrissy out to my parents or in-laws and now, on an evening when I could be doing something with her, I was going out for Chinese food with the lawyer from Hell. I slipped on jeans and a white police t-shirt, just to make the evening quasi-professional. Then I hopped on my bike and headed into Cooksville.

The evening was wonderful. I have always been a sucker for

different cultural experiences. I'd taken a few anthropology courses at university and found them fascinating. They taught me understanding and tolerance, and should be mandatory courses for anyone with a job in the public service.

Dinner was at an old, scuffed-up, wood table in the back corner of a steamy, noisy kitchen. To the background noise of Chinese and the bang of pots and woks, Kelly skilfully prepared for me course after course of delectable and beautiful savouries. We didn't talk much, she was busy cooking and I soaking in all the wonderful sights and sounds around me. The food was hot and spicy, typical of that made in the south of China, Kelly told me. She would prepare a small course and place it on serving dishes and then sit beside me and share until it was time for her to cook the next course. If there was a piece that she thought I should try, she would pick up the serving chopsticks and place it on my plate. I found the act not intrusive, but endearing. I wanted her to use her own chopsticks. Our knees rubbed under the table. I found myself cautiously flirting, and was pleased when she responded. Her chopsticks were red and mine, white.

Christine is the centre of my life. After I left Jimmy Li's Take-Out, I biked to my parents' house; they were babysitting for the night. Tomorrow, I would tell Chrissy all about Kelly and the dinner we'd had. I never talk down to my daughter. She is bright and is starting to recognize words in the stories I read to her at night. I don't want a precocious child, but I do want to give her every advantage I can. The white mayonnaise world is very competitive.

I didn't want to raise her in a subdivision. I wanted her to have the freedom of open spaces like I had as a child before Mississauga spread over the apple orchards and vegetable farms. I had been toying with the idea of moving further north and joining the Ontario Provincial Police or going west and joining the RCMP. Either way, I needed to retrain, and I could be posted almost anywhere. If I was single, that wouldn't matter, but I wanted good schools and a nice neighbourhood for Chrissy to grown up in. Then there was the problem of grandparents who wanted to see Chrissy, and who were so willing to take her so I didn't have to place her in day care. I'd wait another year or so, I had decided, until Chrissy started school before I made any decisions.

That night, Chrissy was asleep on the couch when I stopped in to see her. I changed and washed her quickly and got her into bed. Then, strangely restless, I poured myself some orange juice and settled in on the couch to think. I should been catching a few hours sleep myself; I was working the graveyard shift. Instead, I sat with my parents as if I was a young child again, sipping my juice and watching television. My eyes beat across the screen, but my mind wandered into private places filled with colour and forbidden dreams. When it was time to go, I went and kissed Chrissy good-night, and then rode over to my place to change into my uniform before driving to work in my old Civic. The daughter, the mother, the guest, the police officer: so many roles, which one was me?

When I was a child, Brenda and I used to pretend all the time. An old, dead oak stood at the edge of a small stone bridge over Frog Creek. A knobby branch hung out, so we called it the Hangman's tree. In the deep grasses of the adjacent field, we'd stomp out homes and tunnels connecting them, and then weave stories of mythical princesses and fire breathing dragons. I fell from Hang-man's tree one day and broke my arm. Childhood becomes myth with age. We remember the good and the bad, but none of the con-necting spread that holds the sandwich of our memories together. There are only the extremes. Good and bad. Just as the Sunday school had taught me.

Adult life had taught me that it wasn't all that easy. The man who had killed my husband had been at an office party. He didn't usually drink so much, but he'd been under a lot of stress. His girl-friend and he had been fighting. Probably his friends would not have let him drive, but he had left quietly without anyone noticing, feeling more sick than happy for his overindulgence. He said he never saw Chris, that the sudden flare of lights had blinded him. Once a responsible citizen with a job and plans for the future, he was now in jail having killed a man. There are times I hate him and times I feel sorry for him.

On the edges, there are very good acts and very bad acts. These are easy to define. People, though, fall into the great grey zone between white and black. The myth zone. We play roles or roles are made for us by fate. We are neither good nor bad, black nor white. We are grey mist. Myth.

I dance around the issue for two weeks. To my surprise, I had really enjoyed the company of the lawyer from Hell. Kelly was intel-ligent and capable, and yet very unassuming in her manner outside of the courtroom. She had always wanted to work for the Crown Attorney's Office, she had told me, but needed to article with a big company and work to pay off her student loan first. As soon as she could, she had applied for, and been hired by, the Crown. It had been my luck to be part of the opposition in her last case with a pri-vate law firm. In criminal law, Crown Attorneys, if they are worth their salt, have a lot of political clout, but the big bucks are made in private law firms, defending the guilty. She was good and she could have built a significant practice for herself. I admired her decision to go with the Crown. More than that, I liked her.

Kelly had a neat sense of humour, a nice body, and could cook.

I liked the pride she took in her cultural background, and the fact that she saw no embarrassment in sharing her humble beginnings but rather enjoyed the atmosphere of the busy kitchen. I had too. Her world was very different from mine, but she seemed just as comfortable living in her immigrant world as she did in mainstream Canada. My world was mainstream, but my private drummer had led me to a back room Chinese kitchen. Could we step into an alternative world together? Could there be bells and whistles for us? Was I chasing smoke, or dancing to my drummer? I needed to know.

I had been given tickets to a Maple Leafs game. My former in-laws had a box at the Air Canada Centre that their company used for entertaining. When it wasn't being used, they would give away the tickets to family and friends. The tickets were a free pass to take a chance on the ring toss of love. My on again/off again romance with a fellow cop had ended several months before, when she had dumped me for someone she'd met in a gay bar. She told me my having a child made our relationship too complicated. I'd licked my hurt pride long enough to realize it was pointless. It was time to get back in the game. I gave Kelly a call.

"I was wondering if you are doing anything Saturday," I asked.

"Nothing special."

"I was hoping you'd be free to come to a hockey game at the Air Canada Centre. I was given some tickets. Chrissy is going to spend the day with her grandparents."

"Chrissy?"

"My daughter. She's three. Can you come?"

"Sure."

So, that was a double hurdle overcome. First, she had accepted, and second, she now knew I had a daughter.

It's best to get that bit of information out in the open right away. Love me, love my daughter. We are a package deal, whether it is a casual relationship or something more serious. If Kelly had been surprised or annoyed, she didn't indicate so. There had been only a second's hesitation and then acceptance.

I drove. That's my way. On the way, I told Kelly about Christopher and Christine. She didn't probe, but her few questions got a lot of information out of me. She was good at the cross examination. I learned little about her that I didn't already know. Kelly's personal world was smoke. I suppose she had made herself vulnerable on our first meeting; she had taken me to the root of her childhood. Now it was my turn. The difference was, I revealed the personal while Kelly had revealed the cultural. I knew nothing of her immediate family or her loves.

I could see that she was uneasy, not knowing where she stood with me. She was wondering whether I was gay or not.

"You are confused," I stated.

"Yes. I guess. I'm not sure why you invited me."

"Because I want to get to know you better."

Her face showed she was startled by my openness and unsure what to say.

"I need you to know that I'm gay. It's not just a friendship I'm looking for, and I got the feeling last month when you made dinner for me that there was a possibility that you might feel the same way. Am I wrong?"

"No. You are not wrong. You were married. You have a child."

"Many gay women do."

We talked then about my relationship with Chris. We danced around the issues, not really being completely open but allowing peeks over the emotional walls every now and again. It's a game, just like the one on the rink. We all have our positions, our roles. Someone scores and everything changes briefly, and then returns to the way things were before. All games are the same: positions, the play, the score – if you are lucky, then back the way things were to start again. The game is the same on the field and in real life. We dance. We dance.

I was exhausted by the end of the afternoon, but pleased. Things had gone well. We would be seeing each other again. She invited me in. *How far in?* I wondered. But I needed to get home and spend some time with Chrissy. I was still on the graveyard shift.

A cop shop is a locker room. That's the mentality and that's the atmosphere. If you haven't got the balls and the stomach for the game, then you don't last long. There is one rule: always watch your partner's back. No one wants to ride with a cop you can't count on. Guys don't like riding with women because they are not strong enough in a fight and are too quick to pull a gun. In Canada, cops don't like guns. Pull one, and even if you don't fire it, you'll be facing a pile of paperwork. Cops hate paperwork even more than guns. Instead of guns and arrests, that last as long as it takes to set bail, cops prefer to keep their territory clean with a scorecard. Someone helps you out, and you return the favour when that person needs it. Someone crosses you, you take the troublemaker for a little walk down a dark alley and teach him a little fear. Shocked? Don't be. It's Vic's law. The law of the street. And that's where cops operate – on the streets.

A cop shop is also a store front: neat uniforms and politically correct talk, wine and cheese parties, and standing by the mayor.

We show our wares for the public to buy. It takes a lot of money to run a police force. We dance the political game. The streets are whitewashed to look good for the taxpayer. It is all about cocktail parties and cute little white bread sandwiches with fillings mixed with mayonnaise. We dance.

I was lucky. I was assigned a seasoned cop whose partner had retired. The first week was Hell. He didn't want me and he made that clear. I was a liability. The second week, we were called to a domestic and Gino got jumped by a drunken wife beater with a beer gut, a knife, and overactive sweat glands. I had trained to handle a violent situation, but my upbringing had never prepared me for it. Near panic, I managed to followed procedure and called for back-up. Then I joined in with my nightstick.

I had studied Kendo and Shinto most of my life, and since join-ing the force, had trained for hours with my nightstick. No one uses a nightstick as well as me. On an adrenaline rush from fear, I had the guy down and cuffed before any back-up arrived. A wild punch had caught me in the nose and I was squirting blood, but I still got to read the bastard his rights. My first arrest. In my report, I said I had acted as back-up, but Gino gave me the credit for coming to his rescue.

"You're all right, Squirt," Gino had said. Maybe he was refer-ring to the blood; it couldn't have been my height. I'm five six, a respectable height for a female. Gino is an Italian, who is barely two inches taller than me and has to stand on his tiptoes to see the top shelf of his locker. "All right" is the secret password to the locker room. If you were all right, you were one of the guys. I took a lot of abuse from the guys over my first arrest and the nickname stuck. I was Squirt ever since. Gino taught me so much. Thanks to him, I hope to live to get my pension.

So, as soon as we'd finished our briefing and picked up our squad, I filled Gino in on my afternoon with Kelly.

"Squirt, you damn pervert, you are going straight to Hell." Gino crossed himself and smiled.

I laughed. "Because I like women?"

"Hell no, because you like a woman lawyer! They got a special place in Hell for your kind."

It was a pretty quiet night for a Saturday. It had rained hard and turned cooler, heralding an early fall, so the bad guys had stayed home to watch TV. The bars were quiet, and that meant if we were lucky there wouldn't be too many domestics. No one likes domestics. They can explode in an instant and the officer is caught in the crossfire. We did a tour of the bar district, slowly cruising main street and then checking the back alleys. No gang action tonight. Finished with the bar district, we checked the working corners where the girls and guys sold their wares.

Most had already called it a night or found a Joe who was willing to pay for a dry bed. We stopped to talk to Lacy, a young hooker who was staying out of the rain having a cigarette in a doorway.

"Hey Lacy, how's business?"

"I ain't got no business and neither do you. Leave me alone."

"Where's your old man?" I meant her pimp.

"Around."

"Only the real perverts are going to be out on a night like tonight, Lacy. Be careful."

"Girl's gotta make a living."

"You got that right." We all dance. Gino put the squad in gear and we rolled on.

"Hell, if that was my kid I'd just curl up and die." Gino had three kids — a son in insurance, a married daughter, and a younger daughter still in university. "It's scary having kids today. It's like playing Russian roulette."

I nodded. I wonder all the time about whether I can be a good enough mom to bring up Chrissy so that she will be stable, secure, and happy. It's not easy when you are a single mom, and it's worse when you are bi-sexual. It's a life style that comes with a lot of guilt.

"I'd like to move to a smaller community, somewhere Chrissy can run and play in the countryside."

Gino looked shocked. "Leave Mississauga? They got good schools here, and shopping malls and stuff. Why would you want to move to nowhere? Once, the family rented a cottage up north. The mosquitoes flew in squadrons. The raccoons got in our garbage, too. And when it rained, the power went off! Not that it mattered much. We couldn't get more than a few stations. Honest to God, it was primitive. We never did that again. We put in a pool the next year. There is nothing in those northern towns."

I laughed. Gino is a city boy.

Next, we checked the parks and green spans looking for parked cars. Again the rain had washed opportunities away. I found this duty boring, but Gino took it seriously. Mostly, we'd find young people trying to get it off on the back seat. Gino would put the fear of God into them and send them home. Occasionally, there'd be a minor involved or there'd be a drug deal going on, and we'd make an arrest. We'd pull up behind a car so our lights blinded them. Gino would get out with his heavy duty flashlight and knock on the fogged up windows. I'd sit in the squad with my door open, ready to respond if needed and radio in our position. Usually, Gino would tell them to pull up their pants and get the hell home. Sometimes, I'd see him back up and put his hand on the butt of his gun, then I'd be out in a flash, watching the other doors. Tonight, there was not much going on.

"How about we take a break and get some coffee, Squirt. Then maybe we'll cruise about looking for some traffic violations."

"Sounds good. The bars will be closing soon. We might pick up a few drunk drivers."

Gino nodded but didn't say anything. He knew how I felt about drunk drivers.

"Detail 26, report to a possible 10-44 at 146 Hood." Gino turned the squad around as I picked up and sent an acknowledgement. We were on our way to a possible homicide.

"This your first?"

"Yeah."

"Make sure you go by the book or the courts will make mincemeat out of you. Once we ascertain the situation and call in support, there should be a homicide team there on the scene pretty quickly, but for the first little while it will be just us."

I nodded.

Gino looked over at me. "Be careful."

"You too."

We wove our way through the deserted subdivision streets and pulled up at number 146 Hood. A woman stood on the porch waiting. Our headlights flashed over her as we pulled into the driveway.

"Shit!"

"What?"

"That's Kelly."

"Shit. You stay here and call for back-up. Don't talk to her."

"But–"

"Squirt! Don't you give me any crap. You just do as you're told."

I nodded. Gino was right. My knowing Kelly could jeopardize the situation. I bit my lip and did as I was told. I didn't like Gino going in alone. I was sick with the thought that Kelly might be involved in this and I wanted back-up there right away to get me out of this mess.

I watched Gino go up and talk to Kelly. The two of them disappeared into the house. Only a few minutes went by before Gino's voice crackled into my ear piece. "Looks like a 10-44. Call for a crime team and then get some police tape up around the front lawn."

"Roger that. 10-4." I opened the door and the wind and rain attacked my hot face with ice pricks. It was going to be a bitch of a night. I got the yellow police tape out of the trunk and strung it between two parking signs. The rain had turned to the first snow and was blanketing the darkness in cold white. Two more squads pulled up. The dance had begun.

Their Story Part 1

When I was young, I had been fascinated by shipwreck stories. I had read about all of them sitting at the table in the back of our take-out: the *Titanic,* the *Lusitania,* the *Empress of Ireland,* the *Hood,* the *Bismarck,* and many more. Maybe it was because my father had taken a ship to come to Canada, or maybe it was the romance and tragedy that appealed to me when I was young. Shipwrecks. They were like a capsulized life. They had beginnings, lives, and ends. For a brief while they held the attention of the world, and then faded into time, their destiny changed by a cruel twist of fate. Life is smoke.

One of the events that I had thought a lot about was the dilemma faced by each of the *Titanic* sailors that manned the lifeboats the night of the sinking. Ethically, they had been given command of the lifeboat and were duty bound to get their charges to safety as soon as possible. They had been ordered to make for the ship on the horizon, the *California.* And yet, they could hear the calls of the people in the water crying for help. Each lifeboat had room for more passengers; they had been launched half full, in most cases. Morally, they had a duty to row back and try to pull a few more to safety before the killing cold of the North Atlantic touched their hearts. But the fear was that those dying of the cold would grab at the boats and capsize them if they came near. They sat in the darkness, drifting, sometimes arguing, sometimes silently listening to the voices crying out getting fewer and fewer. In the end, only one boat ventured back, and found none alive.

Usually, ethical and moral decisions go hand in hand. What is ethically right has typically been based on ancient laws on what is morally right. When there is a conflict, however, the choice becomes very hard. I had been trained as a lawyer to believe that justice must be done. If the police did not follow the legal procedure and violated the rights of the accused, then the accused went free. Justice is blind and impartial.

But I was not blind and impartial. I knew I was about to face my own lifeboat decision. I prepared for both outcomes. I knew that the decision one way or the other would rip at my soul. I stopped at the red light, following the law even as I considered breaking it. It was raining hard and the red of the stoplight stained the rain drops on my windscreen the colour of red brick before the wiper erased them away. Life was red smoke. There one beat, and gone the next.

I am myth, both to myself and to others. I know only what I

care to know about myself and others know less. I am myth, and I was the creator of myth.

I pulled up in the driveway of my sister's house and turned off the engine. To the drum of the rain, I pulled on latex gloves before getting out of the car. The wind had got up and the temperature had dropped. The icy hounds of Hell seemed to snap at my heels. If there was a God, I hoped He forgave me, for I was enjoying the excitement and challenge as much as I was dreading what waited beyond the door. I checked my watch for time. Time was my enemy. I didn't use the front door, but took the sidewalk around the back. I ripped the screen away from its frame in the storm door and picked up a rock from the edging to the garden. I broke the glass and reached in to flip the catch. I repeated the process with the glass in the back door. I had to be very careful. The smallest scratch, and my plan would not work. I left the doors open, letting the wind and rain splatter in.

I checked the time. It was my master now.

My sister was sitting in the living room, staring at the wall. She had a large bruise on her arm and a split lip. Jason was on the floor on his side. Knife wounds, fortunately, bleed little on the outside. What blood had drained out of him had been absorbed by the rug. A neat, round, red stain on a white carpet, as if it had been the rug that had bled to death.

It is only then that Sarah looked up. "How did you get in?"

"I heard banging around the back of the house and went that way. The back door has been broken. I came in that way."

"The back door is open?"

"Yes, it's open and banging in the wind. I just came in that way. I left it because the police will want to see it."

"W...What?" My answer has confused her. She got up to look.

"Don't touch anything. Someone must have broken in."

She looks frightened. "I...I didn't hear anyone. Are they still here?"

"No."

"I don't remember anyone being here. Just me and Jason. He tried...he..."

I forced the panic down. Time was passing. "You are in shock. I don't suppose you remember anything correctly. It was probably the burglar who attacked you and then killed Jason. Right?"

"No. I mean, I..."

I repeated slowly and distinctly, "You don't remember any-thing. It is better if you don't remember anything. Bad things are better not remembered. The police will ask a lot of questions. You don't remember anything. It was probably a burglar who attacked you and killed Jason."

She looked at me now. Understanding was starting to creep in past the shock. "I don't remember anything. Nothing."

"Good. I want you to go into Hu's den now while I call the police. Just sit there. Don't do anything, okay?"

She nodded and did as I asked. Quickly, I pulled Jason's wallet from his back pocket and pulled out the cash and put it in my own wallet. I put the wallet aside and squatted by the body and used my gloves to rub the handle of the knife. I could only hope that I had smeared all the fingerprints. I used a nail file to clean under his nails, dropping the scrapings on a tissue and balling them up. Then, leaving the wallet open and his credit cards pulled out, I walked to the back door and heaved the wallet as far as I could into the backyard.

I flushed the tissue and my plastic gloves down the toilet, then checked my watch again. It commands.

I checked on Sarah one more time to make sure she was okay, "Sorry, I felt sick and had to use the bathroom." I needed a reason in case she had heard the flush. "You don't remember anything about the evening, right?"

She looked calmer now, more in control. "No, I don't remember anything."

"It will be a long night with lots of questions. You remember nothing. I want you to use the bathroom now. You might not get another chance. Make sure you wash your hands really well, particularly under the nails. Okay?"

I could see the understanding in her eyes. She nodded and went to do as I directed. I didn't want to disturb the crime scene anymore than I had to. The more changes, the greater the chance of a mistake. I went out to my car and used my car phone to call 9-1-1.

"9-1-1 Emergency Services."

"This is Kelly Li. I am with my sister and brother at my sister's house at 146 Hood. My sister called me. They've been attacked. I...I think my brother's dead. Please, we need help." My voice shook. The cold? Stress? Fear? Acting? It hardly mattered. The tape will be used in court. I closed and locked my car and checked on Sarah one more time. She was back in the den.

"Did you go to the bathroom and wash your hands?" I asked, as if she was a little girl.

She nodded.

"You don't remember anything about the evening?"

She shook her head.

I went and waited by the front door. I needed an excuse for being wet.

The squad came slowly down the street and pulled in behind my car. For a second, I was in the police spotlight. I didn't like the feeling. I was shaking now with the cold. A burly cop got out of the squad and walked over to me.

"You called for help?"

"Y...Yes. My sister called," I looked at my watch as if I didn't know the time, "about t...three quarters of an hour ago. She was hysterical. She said my b...brother was dead. I came over right away. H...he's in there. I made my sister g...go into the den. Except for going to the b...bathroom, she has stayed in there. She needs medical a...attention."

"Step inside, out of the cold."

He wanted me where he could see me.

I did as I was told, waiting in the lobby. The cop went over and looked at Jason then stood and looked around before he talked into his mike.

"Looks like a 10-44. Call for a crime team and then get some police tape up around the front lawn."

He walked back into the kitchen and saw the back door open.

"Was the back door open when you got here?"

I had to pick my words carefully. "I did notice the door was open, yes."

"Did you see anyone?"

"No, just my sister and my brother."

"Your sister is where?"

"I found her sitting on the couch here. She had been beaten and seemed in shock. I told her to wait in the den. She has been there ever since, except to go to the bathroom once." I pointed to the room in question.

The cop looked around. "You go wait in the dining room."

I nodded and again followed instructions. It was up to Sarah now; I had done all I could. I stood in the dark room, looking out the window. It had started to snow. That was good. It would make finding any clues harder. The cop outside was a woman. I watched her tying off the yellow crime tape. For a second, her face was illuminated by the street light. It was Jane.

I felt my guts tighten. It was a night of bad Joss. Bad luck. *How much bad luck?* I wondered. *Enough to destroy us all*, was the answer. The Chinese love to gamble. We bet on horse races and cards, and we love casinos. The stakes were very high that night. It was a game of Russian roulette. Jane must have known I was in there. She could not have failed to see me standing on the porch. She was being professional and keeping her distance. She could not compromise the case. I knew this and turned away from the window. We each had to play our roles.

The crime scene squad arrived about a half hour later, then two ambulances arrived. I looked out the window again and saw others doing the same. They were the curious neighbours, circling like vultures around the excitement of the moment. I was like them. I wanted to be in the thick of things. I had to force myself to remain in the backwater of the dining room. I noted some neighbours had hurriedly put on coats against the first snow of the season and had ventured out in the cold to be the first to know what was going on. I didn't know much more than they did. I waited.

I saw Sarah taken away in an ambulance, an IV in her arm. I wished I could go with her. That wouldn't be possible for a while; I must give all the details to the officer first. I asked if I could contact Sarah's husband, and a detective stayed with me while I phoned. I punched in his cell phone number and he answered sleepily. The sun was rising. I had lost track of time. Normally, I would have spoken in Cantonese, but I didn't want to cause suspicion and so decided to speak English instead.

"Hello?"

"Hu, it's Kelly Li. Sarah is okay, but there has been a serious incident at your house tonight."

"What?" He was awake now. Alert.

"I'm not sure what happened. Sarah called me about two o'clock, hysterical. She told me Jason was killed. I came over to your house. Jason is dead, stabbed, and Sarah had been roughed up. She's okay, but seems in shock. It looks like someone broke in through the back door. You need to get back. They just took Sarah to..." I looked at the cop for guidance.

"Peel," he stated.

"Peel Hospital. You need to be with her, Hu."

"I leave as soon as I dressed. Sarah is okay?" In his fear, his English has failed him. He was a good husband.

"I think so."

"Do parents know?"

"No. I don't want to wake them so late at night. I'll go over and tell them as soon as I am allowed to leave."

The detective wanted to talk to me then. We sat at the dining room table. I felt my soul ripping with the strain. I was alone in a lifeboat, surrounded by blackness. The voices of the dead and living called to me. I showed him my Crown Attorney ID card and gave him my business card with my phone numbers on it.

He nodded. "I thought you looked familiar. You're new, right?"

"Yes. I was hired only a few months ago. I've been with a private firm before this."

"I'm Detective Heinlein. I need to ask you some questions. I want to put it on tape. Okay?"

"Okay."

"For the record, I need you to state your name, occupation, home address, and home phone number." I did this.

"You know what happened here?"

I could answer this honestly. "No." I was trying to answer all the questions honestly if I could. "My sister seemed to be in shock when she phoned me, and when I arrived here, we didn't talk about what happened. I didn't question her. It wouldn't have been appropriate."

He nodded, but frowned. He looked tired and needed now, at the end of his shift, a shave and some sleep. His suit was cheap, worn and wrinkled. He knew I would cooperate to a certain degree, but he also knew this was family. That changed everything. The detective was no fool.

No doubt he was pissed. Who could have blamed him? He'd just drawn a political nightmare at the end of his shift. It meant a double duty and a lot of questions asked from up above. *I was one of their own, one of the good guys. Wasn't I?*

"Your sister phoned you when?"

I checked my watch. I was not sure why. It was a reflex reaction, I guess. "It was just around two."

"What did she say?"

"I can't tell you word for word. She spoke in Cantonese and wasn't making a whole lot of sense. She was near hysterical. She told me that Jason was dead. Killed. I asked her where she was and she said at her home. I then asked her if Hu, her husband, and her boys were there. She said no, that they were on a Scout camping weekend. I asked if she had phoned anyone else. She said no. I told her to sit down and not touch anything and not to answer the door or use the phone until I got there. Then I got dressed and headed over here."

He recorded what I said and took notes as well.

"How come you didn't ask if she was all right or safe?"

Damn. I was taken off guard. "I don't know. I had been sleeping and was shocked."

"Why didn't you tell her to call 9-1-1?"

Things were not going well. Already the detective was seeing holes in my story. "I don't know. I tried to do the right things, but I didn't think to call 9-1-1. I just came over myself."

"Weren't you afraid there might be a murderer here waiting for you?"

I felt my stomach tightening into a knot. "No. I didn't consider that. My sister called for help and I just came."

He nodded. "Okay, you get here, then what?"

"I pulled in behind Jason's car, then walked around to the back door. It was broken open and I walked in. The rain was blowing in and there was glass everywhere, but I thought it best to leave things as they were. I found Sarah sitting on the couch in the living room. Jason was on the floor. I made sure Sarah was all right. She seemed really out of it. She was just staring and not reacting at first. I took her to wait in the den."

"Did she say anything to you?"

"Not much. She seemed in shock. I don't think she knows what happened. I don't think she can remember."

"What did you do next?"

"I checked to see if my brother was dead, then I threw up in the bathroom off the hall. I checked on Sarah again and went out to my car to phone 9-1-1. I waited on the porch until the squad arrived. The police officer told me to wait in the dining room after that."

"What about your sister?"

"She stayed in the den, except to go to the bathroom once. She used the same washroom I did, the one across from the den."

"Where were you this evening?"

"I was with Police Officer Anderson of the Peel Regional Police. We went to the hockey game together at the Air Canada Centre and then had dinner. She dropped me off back at my condo about eight, I did some chores, watched TV, had a drink, and fell asleep in my chair. My sister's call woke me up."

"You didn't go out again?"

"No. Can I go now, Detective Heinlein? I want to check on Sarah and then I'll need to tell our parents. Our father is very old. I don't want him to find out on the news. This is his only son."

He looked up, his eyes meeting mine. I forced myself not to look away. "You don't seem very upset about your brother's death."

I answered honestly. "My brother Jason was raised in Singapore. My sister and I never met him until we were in our teens. You will find that he has had run-ins with the police. He was the black sheep of the family."

"I guess he has some enemies, then. How did you and Sarah feel about him?"

"I'm sure he had enemies. He was not likeable. I was not comfortable around him and avoided him as much as possible."

"Did you hate him enough to kill him?"

"I didn't hate him, I just avoided him. Jason was a loser. Every family has them."

"And your sister, what did she think of Jason?"

"I would have to have her answer that question."

Heinlein nodded. "Thanks, Kelly, for your cooperation. I have all I need for now. I hope your sister is okay. I'll try to get in to take her statement later."

"It's going to be a long shift for you. Take care." I left.

Outside, I had to wait for the okay before the police would take the crime tape down so I could back out of the driveway. The okay came with a condition, and I had to wait some more for the police to search my car. It was not Jane that did it. She stood back, holding a flashlight while another cop checked my car. What were they looking for – another weapon, drugs, a confession taped to my rear view mirror? I waited. The world around me had turned white. I thought about the white rug in the house. The blood stain would have dried by then to the colour of brick red.

"You okay?"

It was Jane. She stood beside me as her colleague went through the trunk of my car

I nodded. "It's been a rough night."

"Your brother?"

Again I nodded. "We weren't close, but this is still a terrible shock. I'm on my way to see my sister at the hospital. She's been roughed up. Then I'll have to go tell my parents."

"Call me later if you need to."

My eyes met hers. "That wouldn't be appropriate."

"I know. Call me." She smiled.

I smiled back.

I stopped to pick up a coffee at Timmy Horton's. The sun was up now and the wet snow was melting back. I had been up for most of the night and I felt stretched to a paper thinness. I sat in my car for a minute and sipped my coffee, letting its warmth spread through me. I caught a glimpse of myself in the rear view mirror. My hair hung limply around my face and my eyes were dark. Strain had etched my face and aged me overnight. I was a wraith. I was smoke. My soul had ripped.

I found my brother-in-law sitting by my sister's bed. He too had aged. "They give her something. She hysterical."

I nodded and placed my hand on his shoulder. "The boys?"

"They at camp. I tell them I must go back because of business. The Scout leader will bring back tonight."

"Has she said anything?"

"Over and over, she say she can't remember. The doctor say she not raped and injuries small, but she have post traumatic shock."

I looked at my sister. She was a little bird tossed from the nest – curled, bony, and grey. My future, her future, our family honour rested on her ability to remember nothing. I didn't need her hysterical or drugged; I needed her clear headed and focussed. The detective was no fool.

I looked at my watch. "I need to tell our parents. I'll be back." I leaned down and gave Hu a hug. "It will be all right." Was I reassuring him or me?

I parked by the tall wall of a red brick building. It is a small condominium building that my father bought. He lived on the top floor with Quin and had an office on the first floor. It was there that I would find him, even at this early hour. My father's life was work. He had created a dynasty to pass on to Jason. It brought him honour.

His secretary was not yet in and I used the code to release the lock to the outer office. "It's Kelly, Father."

"Ah, come in. Why are you here so early?"

He was a small, shrunken figure in a big leather chair. The collar of his shirt hung loose around his scrawny neck and his grey suit jacket slumped off his small shoulders. His eyes were still sharp and alert, though. The mind had outlived the body.

I wished I knew him, but I didn't. He was an authority figure in my life – respected, but not understood. Did I love my father? How could you love what you didn't know? I respected my father for what he had accomplished, for his hard work. I did not trust him. His reality was very different from mine. My father was a myth learned in childhood and barely understood.

"I have very bad news. I have been at Sarah's house most of the night. She called me in the early hours of the morning. Jason was there. I don't know what happened, other than it appears someone broke in the back door. Sarah was bruised, but Jason was stabbed to death. I am sorry, Father."

There was silence. The bright eyes across from me seemed to fade. "Jason is dead?"

"Yes."

"He was to carry on my family name."

"Yes."

"What is the use of good fortune if there is no family to give honour?"

"There is Sarah and myself," I reminded him. He was a wall – cold, rough, unmoving.

He looked at me with angry eyes. "You should have been a boy."

The anger wounded. I tried not to show my pain. I, too, had face, even if I was only a woman. "Is there anything you want me to do, Father? If not, I will go upstairs and tell Quin and my mother."

He growled. "They will be pleased by my misfortune."

I got up and looked down at him with anger. "No one wished Jason dead, Father. Bad things happen."

Again he growled in defiance. "You should have been a boy."

"And you should have seen the woman that I am," I snapped, and left.

It was the last thing I said to my father. When my mother rushed to take tea to him while I sat with Aunt Quin, she found him dead, still sitting at his desk. His red brick world was over.

I do not regret my angry words. In the end, we were honest with each other. A single tear of water is soft and gentle; a raging river is a destructive force out of control. I could never have reached my father, and he could never have seen my pain. We lived on opposite sides of a red brick wall.

Their Story Part 2

My white bread and mayonnaise upbringing did not prepare me for police work. I had to toughen up quickly, having seen things while on duty that lay way beyond the facade of middle-class Canada. Canada the good. In many ways it still is, but there is Canada the bad, too, and it was my job to keep it at bay to give ordinary citizens the feeling that this is a world of safety, peace, and tolerance.

The Li murder was the first I had been involved in. It also involved someone I knew. I took a special interest in it. Statistics show that most murders are solved in the first three days. In cases that take longer than that, the success rate drops off significantly. The Li case had been underway for five days. Most violent crimes are committed not by criminals, but by family members. I knew Carl Heinlein would have first looked for a motive within the family. *Could Kelly kill?* I wondered. Yes, we all could, if put in the right situation.

I was interviewed at the time by Carl.

"You are a friend of Kelly Li's?"

"More of an acquaintance. I only met her recently. Her mother was in a single car accident that I responded to. She had a stroke at the wheel, but recovered. Her mother wanted to thank me for my kindness and so Kelly cooked dinner for me. We had a good time, and so when I was given tickets to Saturday's hockey game, I invited her to go along."

"You drove?"

"Yes."

"Did she seem worried or agitated in any way?"

"No, she was relaxed and happy."

"When and where did you leave her?"

"I dropped her off back at her place a little after eight. She invited me up for a nightcap, but I said no. I needed to get back to see my daughter before I went on duty."

"And you were the responding Officer to the 9-1-1 call?

"My partner and I, yes. Kelly was waiting on the porch. As soon as I recognized her, I told Gino and he ordered me to stay outside. I did not take any direct part in the investigation."

"Did you talk to Kelly or her sister?"

"I talked to Kelly while her car was searched by another officer. I asked if she was okay and she said yes. I asked her if it was her brother because that was what I had heard. She said yes, that they weren't close but that it was still a shock. She told me she wanted to see if her sister was okay, that she had been roughed up, and that she needed to go tell her parents."

"That was it?"

"Yes."

"Have you seen or talked to her since?"

"No."

After my statement, Carl Heinlein read me part of his investigation file. The investigation had found plenty of reasons that someone might want to kill Jason. He was not likeable, and he was the primary heir. He'd had brushes with the law and was associated with a number of rather shady characters. He also had huge gambling debts.

Jason Li's wallet was found on the back lawn, where it appears it was dropped. His credit cards were scattered about, and there was no money in his wallet. There was evidence of forcible entry. The screen door and glass in the back door had been broken using a small rock from a flower bed. Both doors were found open.

The victim was stabbed once and the knife was left in the wound. It was a fish boning knife taken from a set in the kitchen. The assailant was most likely a right handed person. The fatal blow was a downward stroke that slipped between the second and third rib and sliced into the heart muscle. A downward stroke is usually an indication that the attacker was not familiar with the use of a knife as a weapon, however, a single, fatal blow is either very lucky, or delivered by someone who knew what they were doing. The autopsy indicated that the knife might have been pushed further into the victim, either deliberately or due to the impact with the floor. There was evidence of a struggle, however no clear physical traces of a third party were found. The weapon was rubbed clean of fingerprints, as was the body. The victim's body did bear several fingerprints from his sister. They may or may not have indicated a struggle. The time of death has been placed between 10:00 pm and 2:00 am. All members of the Li family are right handed.

The sister also had marks on her body, indicating a struggle. There was no indication of rape, although her clothes had been ripped, indicating that an attempt at rape might have occurred. No fingerprints were found on Sarah although there were bruises indicating that she had been held forcibly. Scrapings taken from under the fingernails of both victims were inconclusive. So far, Sarah has been unable to recall the events of the evening. She is being treated for shock. At 1:48 am Sunday morning, Sarah, called her sister, Kelly, telling her that Jason was dead, stabbed. Kelly found the back door open, entered that way, and found her brother dead and her sister in shock.

Sarah's husband, Hu, and two sons were away on a camping trip. Hu was at the camp at all times and returned only when Kelly called him with the news. Kelly had spent the afternoon and evening with Officer Anderson, and had gone home, done some chores, had two beers and watched a movie on TV before falling asleep in her chair, until she was woken by the call from her sister. The manager of Kelly's building recalls seeing Kelly's car in the parking lot at a little past one in the morning when he returned from the local bar. At that hour of the morning, it is a twenty minute drive from Kelly's condo to her sister's house. Kelly did not place the call to 9-1-1 until 2:33 am. She stated she spent time calming her sister and checking to see if her brother was dead before calling 9-1-1.

Kelly's aunt and mother were with the father for the evening, watching TV. Kelly's mother has lived with Kelly since her stroke, but was staying over at the father's place because Kelly was going out for the evening. None of them drive. There seems to be some confusion as to relationships. Sarah and Kelly have the same father. Sarah's mother is Kelly's aunt and Jason appears to have been adopted. Kelly's mother was not married to her father, but her aunt was. The father had a stroke and died after being told of his adopted son's death.

This last fact caused my heart to contract. Poor Kelly, not only was she dealing with the investigation into the murder of her brother, but also with the death of her father.

Carl Heinlein had read the file to me for a reason. He was not satisfied with the case, and he wanted to use me to get information. I sat by his desk sipping coffee as I listened.

"It's all pretty inconclusive," I said.

Heinlein nodded. "My gut reaction is that one of the sisters knifed him and tried to cover her tracks by breaking the back door, throwing his wallet outside."

"Can you prove it?"

"No. Not unless I can force a confession out of one of them. So far, Sarah is keeping to the story that she can't remember the evening. I have interviewed Kelly several times and her story has remained consistent."

"What does the doctor say about Sarah's memory loss?"

"He said it is extremely likely. He said his patient shows all the signs of severe post traumatic syndrome."

"Could it have been someone else?"

"Yes."

"Kelly?"

"Possible."

"A stranger?"

"Not impossible. Jason had made some pretty scary enemies. It could have been a botched burglary; it could have been a hit. But my gut says no. What was Jason doing at his sister's house at that time of night with her husband away anyway?"

"He could have been checking to see if she was all right there alone, or maybe he was going to ask her for money while her husband was away."

"Maybe."

"But you don't think so?"

"I think Sarah was attacked by Jason and offed him with the boning knife, and then tried to make it look like a break-in. Maybe her sister helped her."

"I don't like the sound of that."

"Neither do I. Sarah has the answers and maybe Kelly does, too. I'll keep working on Sarah. I'd like you to see if you can find out anything more from Kelly."

"You want me to rat on a friend?"

"I want you to keep your ears open and report to me anything suspicious on a murder suspect, Officer Anderson."

I nodded. "Yes, sir." Yes, but not okay. I had been put in an impossible situation. As a cop, I had a duty to report anything I knew that related to the case. As a person, I would be betraying the trust of a friend.

It was two days later when I heard from Kelly. I had tucked Chrissy into bed and was just finishing up our dinner dishes when the phone rang.

"Hello?"

"Jane? It's Kelly."

"Hi. How are you doing? I was so shocked to hear about your father."

"I'm okay, I guess. Ahhh, I was wondering if I could come over for a few hours."

"What is that noise?"

"Buddhist monks. They are chanting for my father and brother so that their good energies can free themselves from the dying personality. They come every day to both our home and to the funeral parlour."

I could hear the tension in her voice. "Come on over."

I met Kelly at the door sometime later and couldn't believe the change in her. She seemed more vapour than substance. She'd lost weight and she looked tired and stressed. "Come in. Come and sit down. You look done in."

"I feel it. There is nowhere to go for any peace."

"What about your condo?"

"My sister Sarah, Hu, and the boys have moved in there. Sarah refuses to step back into the house, and won't allow the boys to go either. She said there are evil spirits there. After the rug is replaced and the back door fixed, Hu is going to sell the place.

According to my sister, the house is built over the eye of a dragon and is cursed."

Not knowing anything about evil dragons, I nodded. I could see why Sarah would not want to go back to the house; she saw a murder there or committed a murder there. I settled Kelly on the couch in the family room with her feet up and a pillow behind her head and went to make some tea.

"How is your sister?"

Kelly frowned. "Getting worse. I'm really worried about her."

"You look like you have been through a really rough week."

Kelly sighed, her eyes closed. "It has not been fun and it is not over yet. The police investigation is ongoing, and so there is no closure for us. A Buddhist funeral takes ten days, so there is no closure there, either."

"You are Buddhist?"

"My father was. I don't practice any faith."

I was interested in this. It was also safe ground. I could ask Kelly questions without entering the smoky ruins of the murder aftermath. "Why ten days? That seems like a long time to keep a body around."

When I brought the tea over, Kelly sat up and some interest came into her eyes. Before she answered, she took a long sip of tea. I settled across from her in the armchair. "Thanks for the tea. I needed it. Buddhism has principals similar to Christianity, but a very different world view. In rural areas, burial takes place usually after three days, but important people, like my father, might not be buried for a year. Special ceremonies would be held on the seventh, fiftieth, and one hundredth days. In the area my family comes from, burial after ten days is common. That's what we decided on. My father was a successful businessman, which is greatly respected in my culture, but more than that he was a scholar. Even at an early age, I can remember men coming to my father's house to ask him how to write a certain symbol. It is fitting that we show respect to him in death."

"And Jason?" The words were out of my mouth before I could consider them. I saw Kelly's face tighten.

"I'm not sure when we'll get his body back. We'll wait three days after the body is released. He will be cremated in a Buddhist ceremony, although I don't believe he was particularly religious."

I nodded, making no comment on the different treatment for father and son. When Kelly talked about her brother, I could hear the contempt in her voice. I danced around the issue. Like a coward, I avoided searching for the truth. I stepped into safer topics.

"What were the monks chanting?"

"It's hard to translate, because some meaning is lost. They say things like: even gorgeous royal chariots wear with time and so does each human body, but the wisdom of Goodness goes on forever and the Goodness reveals itself to those that are good."

"Sort of like a priest telling the family that although the body is dead, the spirit will live on in Christ."

Kelly frowned. "Sort of, but it is far more complicated than that. Buddhists believe that for about four days, the deceased is not aware they are dead. The personality, spirit, of the individual is sort of in a trance. We call this time the First Bardo. The monks chant and pray because they believe that in this trance-like state, the deceased can still hear them and will be directed towards the Goodness."

I tried to make sense of this. "It's sort of a judgment thing?"

"The Buddhist don't judge. A person must seek Enlightenment through thoughts, actions, and deeds. It is a personal journey. Everyone is at their own place. After the four days, the deceased will see a clear light, the road to enlightenment, I guess you could say. Most flee from it, but some are ready and will go on. Those that flee will be reborn."

"Reincarnation?"

"Yes."

"Do you believe that?"

"I don't give it much thought. It's hard enough just living from day to day. Anyway, after the Clear Light, the person starts to realize they are really dead. This is the Second Bardo. It is sort of a time of review and reflection for the spirit, when they see all that they have done and not done in their life. They see their body, yet they now realize that they are not part of it anymore and they start to want a new physical form. The Third Bardo is when the personality seeks another birth based on their level of enlightenment. It's complex."

I smiled. "I can see that."

Intelligent eyes fixed on mine. "I have wanted to come, but I thought it might be awkward for you."

I didn't lie. I wanted her to understand my position. "It is. Anything you say to me I might have to repeat in court under oath. I want to be here for you, but please keep in mind that I'm a cop."

Kelly nodded but didn't say anything.

I filled the silence. "Why don't you have a nap? I promise that there will be no chanting, although I can't guarantee a three year old won't jump on your stomach."

Kelly laughed and leaned back, and I arranged her pillow. Her hands came up to touch my arms and then fall away. I smiled and so did she. There were walls yet to be overcome. I turned down the light, leaving the room in shadow. My new friend was part real, part lost in the twilight of dreams.

My den was white – the undercoat of my life. I used the Net to look up Buddhist rituals. Kelly was right, it was extremely complex. Until that moment, I had never given other religions much credence. Schooled on Sundays, I had believed that faith was a narrow, straight road, one way to Heaven and the other to Hell. When I found that path too narrow to follow, I simply stepped off.

I remember Sunday school as a smell. Sunday school was floor wax, wood, and musty book pages. There was lavender, too. My Sunday school teacher bathed in it, I think, before she slipped into her box suit, pill hat, and white gloves. Her nylon seams were always straight. She was straight – a rod, a switch of authority. Her name was Miss Thornby.

The Church is run by Miss Thornbys. The Church is women governed and controlled by men. Women need faith because they have nothing else, and men need to control women. When women made gains, they left the Church; now the faith is in crisis but still dominated by men. Does the Church respect women? They burned witches by the thousands at the stake. A witch is not black magic, a witch is a woman. The Church burned thousands of women at the stake. The Church opposed as sinful: birth control, abortion, women's liberation, and lesbian rights. The Church has not opposed male enhancement drugs, dead beat dads, men's clubs and gay bashing. If it is a sin to interfere with God's natural plan by taking birth control, why is it not a sin to enhance male performance? Is this not interfering with God's natural plan? If abortion is wasting a life, why is it that men are not damned for not supporting their children? If being an independent woman is sinful because it is anti-marriage, why are men's clubs not sinful? Don't such clubs take men away from the home? Why is gay love a sin, but abusing gays is overlooked?

I am told that the Old Testament condemns homosexuality in two different verses. It also sets out the laws for selling female children into slavery. The Bible was also quoted to prove the world was flat and the sun was the centre of the universe. If Galileo had been a woman, he would have been burned at a stake. If Christ had come out, he would have been an evil cult not a religion.

I remember a day long ago when it was raining outside and the Sunday school room had an added scent of wet wool. I was sitting with Miss Thornby at a small table with the other girls. The boys were taught at another table. I was connecting dots to make a picture of Christ with a sheep.

"Miss Thornby, why didn't Jesus marry?"

"He couldn't marry, Jane. Jesus was sent to us to save our souls. He felt temptation as a man, but His faith gave Him strength to resist."

"Why would He want to resist women?"

"He was above all that. He wasn't like Adam."

Miss Thornby talked in riddles like that. I kind of liked Adam. I like women and apples. I think Jesus probably did, too. But St. Paul helped spread Christianity to Europe, not Jesus. St. Paul was short and ugly, they say, and didn't like women. Christianity can be short and ugly, too, and it doesn't like women.

Miss Thornby liked Christianity. All the Miss Thornbys do. Christianity gives them the male rulebook for judging. Miss Thornbys like to judge and find others wanting. I was found wanting. I asked too many questions.

"Faith defies analysis, Jane. Faith is an act of trust."

"My mother said not to trust strangers."

"Jane! Jesus isn't a stranger. He wants to love you."

I pulled a face. "That's why Mom told me not to trust strangers."

I did not last long in Sunday school. I lacked trust. That made me a good cop, but a poor Christian.

Then again, a good cop would not have had a murder suspect sleeping on her couch. What I knew about Kelly Li then could have been put inside a fortune cookie. I had a good opportunity that night to find a thread that the police could follow to solve the Li case. Instead, I danced around the issue. I didn't want to know who killed Jason Li because I didn't want it to be Kelly.

Life is a dance. You are expected to follow the right steps or you are in trouble. There are a series of dances you must perform and variations are not understood or tolerated. Go off and dance freely and you are ostracized, or worse. Did I want Kelly as a dance partner, then? At the time, I was no longer sure.

There was Chrissy to worry about. Chrissy was the centre of my life. When you have a child, everything changes. That is both wonderful and terrifying, all at once. I had heard some of my friends say that they would be good mothers and do everything right. They bought books and went to classes and watched parenting programs. They dragged their husbands along and insisted that they be a part of the mothering process.

I considered my parents good parents. Any emotional scars they left on my brother and me were more a brand of society's norms than their doing. My mother was there for support and sympathy, but never tried to be my friend until I was an adult. My father was a good provider but didn't nurture my brother and me. He is still not my friend. He is my father, and wouldn't want it any other way. He gave us opportunities and advice and discipline when it was needed. My mother was warm cookies, my father pipe tobacco and newspaper. They were not the model parents of today, but they were good parents. I wondered then if I could do as well. How does one play both roles?

There was no husband anymore in my life. There was just a

black, rainy night where he used to be. It was just Chrissy and me. I had only one wish for her: that she grow up to be independent and strong, and dance to her own drummer not someone else's. Was that possible?

I busied myself with the night chores, folding and putting away laundry, taking out some chicken to thaw for the next day's dinner, and mopping the kitchen floor. Kelly slept on. I wondered if I should wake her or leave her to sleep through the night. I had been putting off bedtime, but I was running out of things to do.

Night fears. I was a child again, afraid of the bogeyman under the bed. What if Kelly was a murderer? Was Chrissy safe if I let my guard down and went to sleep? That fear became an unreasonable monster, filling my gut with ice. I forced myself to think rationally. Even if Kelly was involved in the murder, she had no reason to kill us. The murder was not the killing of a psychopath. It was either a random killing of a botched burglary, or a family affair. It was because most acts of violence are committed not by hardened criminals but angry family members that I worried.

In the end, I let Kelly sleep and got ready for bed, one ear always listening for soft footsteps heading down the hall. I skipped my shower. The act would have left me too vulnerable. I checked on Chrissy, asleep in her room, and closed the door softly. Then, on impulse, I went and fetched her and put her limp, warm figure in my bed. I wanted her close so she would be safe. I wanted her close so I would feel safe. Night fears.

My Story Part 2

Every murder case starts at home. That's what they teach at the police college. Whether directly or indirectly, murder starts around the family table. Over 80% of all murders are committed by a close family member or friend, and the remaining cases often started out with rotten family lives. The police will tell you that if you understand the family, nine times out of ten you'll have a pretty good idea who should be wearing the steel bracelets.

That works well on paper, but Southern Ontario is one of the most culturally diverse areas in the world. According to the UN, there are over six hundred ethnic groups living in the Toronto area, making it the most cosmopolitan city in the world. Generally, they get along okay, but big city problems and gangs are starting to undermine that success. Each and every one of those cultures has its own world view and values, and few of them like cops.

My family was first generation Chinese, one step away from the old country's soil and one thought away from old country thinking. That made my week both harder and easier. It was easier because I could shrug my shoulders and explain to the police that my family did not understand. It made it harder because I couldn't count on members of my family reacting the way I thought they should. As soon as they saw a cop, they clammed up and buried themselves in the sand. I'd forced my family to be fairly cooperative, if you consider it cooperative for them to state over and over that they didn't know anything that would help solve my brother's murder.

I knew the police thought that the whole set-up smelled of rotten fish. What was my brother doing at my sister's in the early hours of the morning? Who broke in the back way? Who beat up on my sister, and who killed my brother? Was it the same person? I was asked these questions in one form or another a hundred times that week. Every detail of my statement was scrutinized. Nine times out of ten, a burglar will run rather than fight. The police knew this. The evidence at the crime scene did not make sense. The truth kept swimming away into shadows.

The smell of the fishy deception was a poisonous vapour that rose from the corpse and permeated our clothes, entered our nostrils and seeped into our minds and souls. Everyone touched by the murder was contaminated by it. It was a stench that didn't leave. I sensed its foul odour on me and it revolted me. I'd hesitated about visiting Jane. I hadn't wanted the hideous fumes to touch her, but I needed sleep and comfort and I had nowhere else to go.

I was jumpy and scared. The life I had worked for hung by a

thread. I was asked to visit my mother and aunt with Heinlein and a Chinese interpreter, in case he was needed. My mother said little. When Heinlein started asking her questions, her lips puckered up in a tight button and she rocked back and forth in her chair.

Heinlein was polite. "Mrs. Li, I'm sorry for your family's loss. Perhaps you could help me to understand Jason better. Do you know who his mother is?"

"I have had two strokes."

"Mrs. Li, would you know where we could find Jason's birth certificate, landing papers, or passport?"

"I don't know. Jason should have such things. Talk to him."

"Jason is dead," I reminded my mother. "Detective Heinlein is trying to find out why. Do you know who Jason's mother was?"

"If you had been a boy, none of this would have happened. I don't know about Jason. I have had two strokes. Strokes bad for your head."

A little later, I walk Heinlein to the door. "I'm sorry. It's not just that you are police; I don't think she knows."

Heinlein nodded. "What about you? You know anything about this son that suddenly showed up?"

I shook my head. "I was young at the time and didn't really question his arrival. My sister is older and might know more."

"I'm having trouble here figuring out your relationship with your brother and sister."

He looked me in the eye and I answered honestly. "My Aunt Quin, who really is no relation to me, is my sister's mother and my father's wife. My mother is my father's mistress."

Heinlein couldn't stop the smile from showing, although he tries. "Your dad lived with his wife and mistress? I gotta give him credit. Not many men can pull that off."

I blushed, although I didn't want to. "My father wanted a son to carry on his name. He was old and his world was very different from ours."

"And Jason?"

I sighed. "Jason was the son. He was raised in Singapore. I assume his mother is from there. I know nothing of her." I picked my words carefully. I did not want to lie, but I could not tell all the truth. These sessions are a landmine of words.

"Did your dad go to Singapore often?"

"Not since I have been aware, but this happened many years ago. I know he did go back to China once and brought my mother back."

"Is your mother here legally?"

"Of course. She is a Canadian citizen." This came out like a growl, although I hadn't meant it to. I was worried that maybe my mother's papers were forged.

Heinlein held up his hand. "Easy, Counsellor. I am not with Immigration. I'm just trying to get a handle on the situation here so I can find out who killed your brother."

I bit my lip and fought for control. "Sorry. This has been a hell of a week."

He nodded. "Let's go see your aunt."

My Aunt Quin was no better when we visited her in the kitchen. Her face was set in anger and her eyes were red from lack of sleep rather than crying.

"I am Mrs. Li. Jimmy was my husband. Kelly killed him. She is very bad. You punish her."

Heinlein looked confused. "What?"

"Kelly tell him that his son is murdered. Then he dies. She kill him."

I said nothing. What she said was true enough.

"Mrs. Li, I'm sorry about your husband. He was an old man and I guess his heart couldn't take the shock. The autopsy showed he died of natural causes. Heart failure. Miss Li didn't kill him. I can't punish her for telling her father the truth."

Aunt Quin folded her arms across her pot belly and sat in stormy silence after that. She refused to say anything other than she knew nothing. If I wasn't going to be punished for her husband's death then she simply was not going to co-operate with the police. Heinlein gave up after a while and I walked him to the door.

"You've got your hands full with those two," he conceded.

A smile touched the corner of my lips. "They don't trust the police and I'm afraid their world view is very much the old beliefs of China."

He nodded again and looked at me thoughtfully. For a minute, I thought he was going to say something, then he thought better of it and left. I went and sat on the balcony for awhile. What was Heinlein thinking? What evidence had been gathered from the house? Had I covered my tracks? Would Jane know anything? These questions haunted me. Holding such a secret was like knowing you were being stalked. Everything you said and did might be watched. The police were out to get those that were guilty of this crime. They were after my sister and me.

I was not with him during his interviews with my sister. I was not needed. I was allowed to be there when my mother and aunt were interviewed only because they are old, Chinese, and their English was not very good. I was very worried about what my sister might have said to Heinlein. I had visited with Sarah twice that week, and was shocked to see the rapid deterioration in her mental state. Reality is elusive and easily lost on the winds of change.

When I visited my apartment where my sister's family was staying, it was strangely quiet and my nephews uneasy. My brother-in-law did not look like he had slept. I know he had not been back to work. He ushered me into my bedroom where Sarah sat by the window.

"Hi, Sarah."

No answer.

"Sarah, it's Kelly."

She turns to me now with sunken, dark eyes. "I don't remember," she whispered.

I smiled sympathetically. "I know you don't. Is that what you told the police?"

"Yes. Now I tell you what I saw."

"I don't want to hear." I spoke sharply. It is best I don't know. But she doesn't seem to hear.

"Jason had come to visit. He fell asleep on the couch. I let him sleep instead of sending him home. Then someone broke through the back door. I ran to the kitchen and grabbed a knife, but the bad man took it from me and knocked me down and killed Jason. It was terrible! We can never go back to that house. It is built on the eye of a dragon. It is bad luck. Bad luck."

I blink, not understanding what was happening. "Someone broke into your house? How?"

She grew agitated with me. "You saw. I showed you. The bad man broke through the back door. I heard the glass break. I tell the police. I get the knife from the kitchen, but someone else stabbed Jason. I tell them the house is a bad house. My son broke his arm in the backyard, and my husband caught pneumonia our first winter there. It is a bad house, built on the eye of a dragon. I realize that now. Now a bad person has broken in and hurt me and killed Jason with my fish knife."

I felt my heart pounding. Did Sarah believe this, or was she elaborating on what I had told her? How much of this had she told the police?

"What did the bad man look like?"

"He bad. He was a little black serpent dragon, and his eyes were hot coals and he breathed fire."

I closed my eyes. I can just imagine how Heinlein would react to that. "You couldn't see his face?"

"No. I saw only a little black dragon."

"He wore a dragon mask?"

She looked at me suspiciously. "I tell you what I see in my dreams. I don't remember anything. I don't remember anything."

Sarah rocked back and forth her hands covering her face. Sobs shuddered through her small frame. I went to her and knelt, holding her close. The poisonous vapours were spreading.

After, I sat and talked to my brother-in-law. The doctor had told him that Sarah was suffering from a severe case of post traumatic syndrome.

"Do the police understand this?" I wanted to know.

"Yes. Kelly, do you think Sarah could have killed Jason?"

I felt my heart contract in fear. "Why would you ask that?"

Hu seemed to crumble into old age before my eyes. A once new monument to the successful immigrant, he is now rubble. Invading fears have scaled his wall of defence and shot burning arrows of doubt into his mind. The smoke of war within his heart stinks of Jason's death.

"John...he looks like Jason. I always thought maybe... Why was Jason there? He never visits. Sarah hated him you know. Hated him. She told me so often. I think...I think Jason had raped her."

I felt the cold sweat of horror paint itself across my flesh. I felt naked and vulnerable again, wrapped only in the bath towel of my innocence. I don't want to be having this conversation. "You probably shouldn't be telling me this."

"No, no, I need to tell someone. Sarah had nightmares. She would never talk to me about them, but sometimes she would talk in her sleep. She would cry, 'Jason no! Jason no!' I hated him too. He stole my honour."

"Hating doesn't lead necessarily to murder."

"No, but why has Sarah gone mad? The boys are afraid of her."

I put my hand on his shoulder. "She'll get better. You must be strong for her. Have you told the police any of this?" I tried to make my question sound natural. It was not. It was a question rooted in fear and guilt.

"No. I do not want Sarah in trouble."

"Good. It's best just to tell the police what you know. It is not good to speculate. It simply muddies the waters for the police."

"The doctor feels that Sarah might have suppressed what happened. He thinks maybe the dragon is just a wall she has put up between her and what really happened that night. He thinks maybe Sarah can't face the truth." Hu looked at me, waiting for a response. I didn't give him one.

Hu pressed, looking at me with eyes needing reassurance. "Do you think Sarah killed Jason?"

"I think Jason was roundly hated by a lot of people. Beyond that, I am leaving it to the police to solve this case. That's their job, not mine. Hu, you have enough to deal with. Don't go borrowing trouble with idle speculation, okay?"

He seemed reassured by this. I was not sure why, except that he needed to be. I was not reassured. I was terrified for my sister, my family, and for me.

The monster that Sarah feared was shared by me. I, too, didn't want to face the truth of that night. Instead, she and I had created a new truth, one we could live with. In this truth, an unknown villain stepped between us and the guilt and kept us clean. I wondered if we repeated the story long enough if it would become truth in our hearts. I hoped so. I had heard it was true. Then, the cold realization of what we had done gripped my heart with fear. What had the secret done to Sarah? What demons were tearing her apart?

The truth was it was not the demon of hate that made Sarah kill. What we feared most and what must be buried very deep with as many lies as possible was that the two of us had been raped by our brother. If we were forced to talk about the murder, we would also have to talk about the shame of our rapes. That could never happen.

Then, and still now, society plays at caring about abuse against women, but the reality is very different. Jason was the male hero of the house, brought down by two desirable women. He would have been the victim, and the shame of being ruined would have been ours. Laws do not change social belief, and social belief is a male animal, so are the courts.

It was the next day that I went to see my boss.

"I'm glad you came, Kelly. I've needed to talk to you."

"This is difficult."

"I'm sure."

"I would like to ask for a leave of absence."

He looked at his hands and said nothing for a few minutes. "That might not be enough."

A cold chill seeped over me.

"This office cannot come under question, and neither can those that work for it. The Chief of Police has been in touch with me at the advice of her investigative officers. She has concerns."

I nodded. "You mean I'm a significant suspect in my brother's death."

"I'm not about to comment on an ongoing investigation, but you wouldn't be asking for a leave if you didn't realize that your...situation...is affecting your position here."

I swallowed. Fear was a thousand knives within my heart. "Am I fired?"

"No, no, of course not, Kelly. You are innocent until proven otherwise, especially here." He smiled weakly at his own joke.

I did not smile. I have no reason to make it easier for him. "Then?"

"I've issued a suspension without pay until this mess can be sorted out."

He handed over the papers. They were signed yesterday; my fate decided before I'd had my turn at defence. So much for innocent until proven guilty.

"I'll get my things."

"No."

I looked at him. He pressed a button and stood. "Security will escort you off the property. If you need to return for anything, you will need to make an appointment and return under guard after hours."

I nodded. There was nothing else to say. I left with a security officer.

Shaky and scared, I hadn't been able to make myself go back to my parents' house where my aunt and mother wailed in sorrow to show honour to my father. On the day he was to be cremated, they would hire professional wailers too. I'd gone to Jane's, even though I had promised myself that I wouldn't. I had gone. She had asked no questions, but had bedded me down on her couch.

I woke in a pool of light, feeling warm and secure. The feeling lasted only a second, and then I was confused and baffled by my surroundings. Fear rushed into my soul. I am a young teen once more and it is Saturday morning. I wake with a start and feel for the knife. Its warm, smooth handle is reassuring, but not enough to conquer my fear. I can never lie in. I must get up and dress. I must never be caught vulnerable again.

Still half awake, my hand slipped under the pillow on the couch for my knife. It was not there. I woke instantly and sat bolt upright, cold sweat and fear making me shiver.

"Hey, you're awake. Do you want a coffee?"

I turned and saw Jane. I managed a weak smile although inside my heart pounded. How many years would I have to wake like this before I could put that one evening of horror behind me? Would a thousand years be enough? A million? Could the universe whirl through endless darkness for infinity before my soul would be free? For three years after, I slept in the same bed where Jason had raped me. I bought a new mattress and sheets with my first pay cheque, but in my mind, the scent of Jason's sticky wad still clung to the bed. I would wake each morning in fear and loathing, and rush to wash his scent from my flesh and dress against his attack. My only protection and comfort, the thin edge on which my sanity balanced.

Had Sarah felt the same? Probably. Why had I never asked? Why had she not asked me? Our shame was a lock that kept us chained to Jason's abuse. A fish boning knife had been my protection. Had a similar knife brought my sister her escape? In a way, I envied her. She had done what I had only fantasized about doing.

"Hey, you awake? Do you want coffee?"

"Yes, thanks. I'll just go wash up."

Jane's house was light and laughter. The walls were an off white, and the windows big and covered with shears. Chrissy and I played with her blocks on the floor while Jane quietly sipped her coffee. For brunch, we had chicken salad sandwiches. The mayonnaise was warm and creamy on my tongue. I wanted more: more of this; more of Jane.

We took Chrissy for a walk in the park and played hide and seek in the new snow. Then we sat bundled close on a bench and talked while Chrissy played in the toddler playground.

"She is a nice kid."

Jane beamed. "I'm proud of her. It hasn't been easy working shift, but both Chris's parents and mine have been very supportive."

"That's good."

A frown crossed her face and she watched Chrissy with worried eyes. "Chris's parents would like to sell, now that they are retired, and move to Vancouver. They have family out there and my parents have a trailer in Arizona that they hardly ever use. I feel that they are missing out on their retirement years because of Chrissy and me."

"I don't suppose they mind."

She looked at me and smiled. "No, they don't mind, but I do. I've often thought of moving out to British Columbia. You know, to a smaller town where the pace is slower and there is fresh air and lots of nature for Chrissy and me to enjoy."

"Why don't you?"

She shrugged. "Lack of nerve, I guess. I'd have to retrain with the RCMP, and I can't afford to do that really. But it's not just that, it's leaving Chrissy's grandparents behind when they have been so supportive. Leaving my friends, and, of course, just the hassle and cost of such a move."

I nodded in understanding. I didn't want Jane to move. "It would be hard to move once Chrissy starts school."

She smiled. "Well, I have a few more years before I have to worry about that."

Back at Jane's house, I phoned my mother to make sure everything was okay while Jane got Chrissy ready for an afternoon nap. The phone call left me tense. The smoke of incense seemed to curl like a snake from the phone and enter my ear to worm its way through my organs. The snake was guilt, and its scales rasped against my guts as it slid deeper. I knew I couldn't stay much longer in this cocoon of calm. I was needed to help my family through this difficult time while my father and brother were in the Bardo state.

Jane's arms slid around me. "You okay?"

The pent up tension I was feeling slid low between my legs.

Snake guilt became snake passion, its venom hot and bitter. I turned in Jane's arms and the kiss that followed was demanding. Her response was immediate. The venom spread between us and set us on fire. We were out of our clothes and into her bed quickly. We were mad lovers, driven by hunger to consume each other in a hot fever of need. The sweat coated our bodies that entwined together in the sweet agony of climax. Fever heals, and kills. We laid exhausted in each other's arms, the snake dead and the fever broken.

When I think back on that afternoon, I'm not sure what broke the wall of inhibition between us. It might have been the loneliness that we both felt that or perhaps the ache of the heart needing to be loved, or maybe it was just the lust for physical satisfaction. Perhaps it was all these things. Who knows, perhaps it was love. Such emotions are smoke on the wind, billowing one minute and blown away the next. All that mattered then was the wall of social acceptability between us had been penetrated with groping, eager fingers.

"You okay?" I asked.

"Yes." Her head rested on my shoulder and I felt her warm breath against my naked breast. I shivered.

"You?"

I kissed her forehead. "I'm okay. I'll have to leave soon. My family needs me."

She rolled away and lay on her back. The sheet was folded around her knees and she was naked for me to see. I felt my desire aching low in my pelvis. She was beautiful. The cream of her excitement, pumped to the surface, lay caught in the web of her silk pubic hairs. I bent and kissed her there, tasting her desire once again.

She sighed. "Don't. It's not fair when you have to go."

I didn't feel like being fair. Instead, I ate my fill and she came on my tongue. Later, we showered together. The sticky scent of sex was replaced by peach body lotion. It was a female moment – wet and warm. A heady moment that was comfort.

Kelly brought colour into my life. She was, despite her conservative exterior, a passionate lover and a fun-loving friend. I hadn't meant to make love to her that first afternoon, but I certainly didn't regret it. How could I?

Learning about Kelly was like learning about Canada again. I had grown up in an English textbook of Canadian history. It was British, dog-eared with their natural superiority over the savages, French Habitants, and poor immigrants. I knew little about their stories. Now I was coming out, seeing Canada through the eyes of the thousands of immigrants who have made the nation grow

She had showed me the book of Buddhist prayers put together in honour of her father. On the cover was a pearl and I asked her the meaning.

"The pearl is the Heart Essence of the Buddha. The purity of his essence is enlightenment and that is symbolized in the pearl. The pearl is seen as a living jewel that radiates its purity just as Buddhism is seen as a living faith of compassion and joy."

How different this was from my Sunday school of floor wax and musty books. Christ on the cross hung over us. Christ died for us. There is the cross, the implement of torture to prove it. We are saved, but our guilt for His sacrifice was taught to us from an early age. I suppose our pearl, our heart essence, comes from the acceptance of Jesus and His Word. Still, where is the joy and compassion for me? Me, a gay woman. They love me, I'm told. They will help me see my sin and give me the strength to fight temptation. They will help me be normal, like them. I have walked this walk to the altar of marriage and respectability. I was happy on the outside, but so, so sad and lonely within.

The three of us did many different things together: a trip to the zoo, the art gallery, a hockey game, and the Royal Ontario Ballet to see the Nutcracker. It was a time of adventure, learning and exploring. Inevitably, we would end up back at the Li take-out around the worn table in the back of the old kitchen for our meal. At first, I wondered at this, then I realized that Kelly was sharing with me and my daughter. She wanted us to remember the smells, sights, and sounds – the texture of her Chinese-Canadian world. She was making my daughter and me part of her Canada. She was making a bond.

A bond. That can restrict or add to a relationship. No, not a relationship, not yet. We were still in the discovery stage, that age old dance. One, two, three, Kelly, Chrissy, and me. One, two, three.

Kelly was like a pearl. The immigrant irritant under the respectable shell of the Canadian Establishment. Each year, a new layer formed. Each year, that layer was sealed forever behind the facade of yet another smoky luminescence. Kelly was layers. Walls.

A few nights after Kelly had shown up at my house, we sat curled together on the couch watching the log I'd put on the fire burn slowly down. It was a hard maple log, a branch from a neighbour's tree that had to come down. It burnt slowly and filled the room with a sweet, smoky scent.

"Kelly?"

"Hmm?"

"I need to know, but I don't want to know. If I know, I have to tell the police. If I don't know, I could be sleeping with a murderer, exposing my daughter to her..."

"I didn't kill my brother, Jane." She was relaxed, almost drowsy when she made this statement, her voice quiet and calm.

I snuggled closer, feeling safer at first then wondering how good a liar she might be. The murder was a wall of bright red between us. Could that ever change?

Later, I walked her to the door. "You could stay overnight," I volunteered.

She shook her head. "Can't."

"Why?"

Her eyes were black in this light. Wells of darkness. "Because you want to believe that I didn't kill my brother, but you are not sure."

I was defensive because her words were true. "We've slept together. It's a bit late for me to be worrying about that."

"I can't sleep unless I have my knife under my pillow."

Her words froze me against the wall. The walls were painted the colour of eggshell. I suddenly sensed how fragile my world was. How vulnerable. "A knife?"

"I've had it there since I was a teenager. It has no connection to the murder of my brother, but connections would be made anyway."

"You've told me."

"Yes, I want to trust you. Will you tell?"

"No, not if it isn't evidence."

"It's not. Besides, I can deny this conversation ever took place. Once you saw the knife, it would be different."

I nodded. "Why can't you sleep without it?"

Tears welled in her eyes and ran down her face. I waited, watching the struggle within her play across her face. *Will she tell me?*

"I was raped."

It was a sob that cracks open a dam of emotion. I hugged her close and we slid to the floor, leaning against our eggshell walls. She told me no more. Uttering those three words have left her exhausted. Together, we rocked in the corner of the room. Women. Victims. Women. One, two, three, Kelly, Chrissy, and me.

We never talked about that night again. Kelly left hours later, crumpled and exhausted from crying. I was left with a minefield of emotion, shock, sadness, rage. Rape is not just being victimized, it is having your soul ripped from you. Rape is an infected wound that can only heal on the surface. To know Kelly is to know her pain and to have to deal with it every day. I hoped maybe now that she had pierced the scab of silence and let the green pus of guilt and pain drain out, she would be able to sleep without fear.

There was another set of emotions I was dealing with too, suspicion and confusion. Who raped Kelly? Was it her brother? Had he sexually abused his sisters? If so, this was a very strong motive. Kelly had said that she had not murdered her brother. Did I believe her? Was I now withholding vital information to solving the case, or was I protecting Kelly from being victimized again?

My family. Kelly's family. Contrasts. I am embarrassed to admit that when I had Kelly and my parents over for dinner one night, it was the first time that we had a family meal with someone who was not white. All through my elementary schooling in the 1950s, I had never had anyone from a visible minority in my school. In high school, there had been a few, but not many, and none in my classes. Later in university, as the cultural make-up of Ontario changed, I finally started to meet and socialize with visible minorities, but to my shame, I had never invited any of them home.

If my parents were surprised by Kelly being there, they did not indicate so during the evening. My dad and Kelly got on very well, discussing the economy, and my mother was impressed by Kelly's success and education. It wasn't until the next day, when I went to pick Chrissy up after my shift, that the questions came.

"Chrissy seems very fond of Kelly. You have been spending a lot of time together?"

"Yes."

My mother looked worried and played with the string of pearls around her neck. "I'd heard...I mean...I... There were comments and things I noticed about that Victoria person you worked with when you were at university. I hoped it was a phase. When you married Chris, I thought all that nonsense was behind you." When she met my eye, I saw anger in hers.

"No, nothing had changed. People don't change. What happened was I caved in to the social pressure and married."

She was too agitated to sit then and paced about. "It must end, Jane. What will people think? It's bad enough that you are a police officer, now this." Tears rolled down her face. "What kind of mother are you being for Chrissy? Have you no shame?"

"I'm an excellent mother, who will teach my child to judge people by their character and actions and not by their colour, religion, politics, or sexual preferences." Later, I felt very sad for the pain I caused her, but then I felt nothing, insulated by my own wall of shock and anger.

"For God's sake, Jane, I am begging you, don't get involved with this woman. Do you know her brother was murdered? Murdered! Only a few weeks ago. What kind of family is this?"

"Yes, I know. I was one of the responding officers. Kelly is not involved in the murder, Mom. It looks like it might have been a burglar." Even as I said it, I knew it wasn't true. Kelly was involved; I just didn't know how deeply.

"I think you'd better leave, Jane."

"Okay."

"Jane?"

"Yes?"

"Your father and I will always love you, but we will not support you in this course of action."

"I understand."

So, my perfect world of white bread and mayonnaise went sour. My life was found to be off. What could be worse than a daughter that did not fit the cookie cutter pattern of womanhood and mother?

Then there was Kelly's family. Where mine was like a black and white film, Kelly's was a kaleidoscope of colour and noise. Several times, I had visited her family apartment to show respect for her father and brother while the prayers had been said to help them accept their death and find their way. The impressions in my mind are of orange cloth, incense, brass chimes, chants, and cigarette smoke. People came and went, offered food and support. I felt welcomed because though they talked in Chinese, which I didn't understand, they included me with their eyes. I was accepted. I was part of the colour.

We visited after the cremation, too. When it was time to go, Kelly's mother would stand on her tiptoes and hug first Kelly and then me. Once when I brought Chrissy, she was given a sandalwood fan to take home and a red silk shirt. Kelly's family flowed over me in a wave of humanity. Jealousy, love, respect, anger – the natural jetsam and flotsam of a sea of family interaction washed up at my feet.

"Kelly?"

"Yes?"

"Does your family know that you are gay?"

"No. Maybe yes. We have never talked about it. It would bring us shame to do so."

"How do you explain me?"

"You're my friend. At the moment, my father's passage is the only thing of importance. I imagine there will be questions and accusations down the road. What about your family?"

I bit my lip. Emotion, a sudden flash flood poured through my body. I fought for control and was pleased that my voice sounded normal when I spoke. "There have been questions. My mom, I guess, suspected that I'd been in a relationship with a woman at university. She has never mentioned it before."

"She doesn't approve?"

"Of course not. It's not normal in her world. My parents won't be able to hold their heads up at the bridge club." My voice was laced with sarcasm.

"I don't want to cause trouble for you."

I shrugged. "I'm gay. I've tried being straight and it wasn't me. I don't mean to get involved with a man again."

"Will your family come to accept that?"

Then the tears came, in wrecking big sobs. Kelly held me close. "I don't know. Mom told me that they will love me, but they won't support me."

Kelly said nothing; she just held me. What was there to say? We are the lepers of the 21st century. The Religious Right would have us wear bells and call out, "Unclean". The Righteous Ones. The Godly Ones. Our judges.

We are the circus in the bazaar on the edge of society. Jesters mocking the Word. Our faces whitened by a thousand deaths, we are clowns scorned and laughed at by those who know so much better than us what we feel because they are the normal ones. Our critics.

In uniform, I felt more in control of my life. The rules of conduct, of procedure, of the locker room, of the streets provide the melody of my day. I hummed along with Gino to the rhythm of the squad engine and the static of the police radio.

"So, you still seeing Kelly"

"Yeah."

"You are gonna burn, Squirt."

"Is that a religious observation?"

"Nope, that's an observation that you don't let the fish nibble at your line unless you are planning on hauling her into the police net."

I laughed. "Aren't you full of poetic imagery this morning,

Officer Travenetti."

"You know what I mean, Squirt. You're playing with fire."

"Kelly didn't murder her brother."

"You know that or hope that?"

I didn't answer. He already knew the answer.

Back at the station there was a message for me to see Detective Joel Heinlein. Gino gave me "the look" and went to the locker room. I headed upstairs. I found Heinlein in his cubbyhole office.

"Eh, Anderson, good to see you. Pull up a chair."

"Thanks."

"So, word has it you are still seeing Kelly Li and becoming pretty chummy." The smile he offered was cold, close to sarcastic.

"Yes."

"So? You wanna share anything with the good guys?"

"I haven't identified the killer, if that's what you mean. The family seems genuinely cut up about the death of Mr. Li." I shrugged. "No one was particularly upset about Jason's death, although they went through the motions of seeing him off to a new life."

"Eh?"

"They're Buddhists. You know, reincarnation."

He shook his head. "There is some weird shit out there." He looked at his hands for a few seconds, thinking. "You gotta maintain your objectivity in this job, ya know." He looked at me then. "You're going to find in policing that a lot of good people can do some pretty bad things. Even your friend Li."

"She told me that she didn't kill her brother."

He looked at me with thoughtful eyes. "She tell you anything else, Anderson?"

That was it. I knew I was ethically bound to tell Heinlein what Kelly had related about the knife she kept under her pillow. "No, nothing else. Kelly is a lawyer. She is not likely to share any information carelessly."

"She is also bound by the laws she serves." Heinlein's eyes flashed with annoyance. "And so are you. Remember that, Anderson."

"Yes, sir."

He smiled and leaned back more comfortably in his chair. "I think we'll have an arrest soon. I'd have liked to move earlier, but upstairs wanted to be politically correct and wait until this funeral thing was over and people had got through mourning. Ya know, showing good will to our Chinese community. This Li guy was a real big shot, I guess. He had bunches of money."

"Really?"

"Yeah, why?" The eyes were sharp, alert, like a fox's.

"They live pretty simply in an apartment in a building that Mr. Li owns. Kelly rents a small one bedroom in town, and the sister has a middle-class subdivision house. Nothing special. Kelly worked her way through university. She said her dad has a couple of buildings, but they're all mortgaged to the hilt and there is very little discretionary income."

Heinlein laughed. "That's just one of the lies she has told you. The old man has millions salted away."

Shock rocked me to the core. "What are the other lies?"

He smirked at me. "Wait and see, Officer Anderson. You're gonna learn a lot about being a police officer by watching the master here."

"Yes, sir. Can I go?"

"Yeah. But you just keep in mind what side you're on, Anderson."

I looked him square in the face. "I'm a police officer. I know what side I'm on."

"Good. Good."

I managed to get out of there with some dignity, but I had been badly shaken. Had Kelly been sharing my bed and playing me for a fool?

I changed and headed out to my car. To my surprise, Gino appeared from nowhere.

"We gotta talk. Meet me at the park." He walked away before I could give him an answer or ask any questions.

When I pulled into the park that was on our patrol route, I found Gino leaning against his car, his jacket collar up against the wind. As soon as I stopped, he opened the passenger door and slid in.

"What's up?"

"I did some checking around. You know I got a cousin who works clerical upstairs. Heinlein has issued a warrant for Kelly's arrest. Seems they found some plastic gloves she wore at the scene that night. She must have tried to flush them down the toilet, but they got stuck."

It took me a minute to respond. "Shit."

"Jane, I'm not going to ask how you are going to use this information, but I'm telling you as a friend, distance yourself before the crap hits the fan."

I ran a hand over my face. "Thanks, Gino. Thanks. I owe you one."

Gino nodded and was gone.

I felt numb, frozen like the land. In the winter time, the dark comes quickly. The park was covered in a crusty layer of ice. The branches of the cold, bare trees spread gnarled fingers across the glow of the city sky. I shivered. Death walked over my grave.

I had chosen to hear the music of romance and accept the dance with the masked stranger. I saw the macabre warnings, but ignored them as I laughed at the devil of the Mardi Gras. Now my partner's mask had been removed and I was looking at Hell itself. I opened the door and threw up. The dry heaves my hang-over of emotion.

When it was over, I wiped the mask of frozen tears from my face and swallowed the bitter bush taste. I drove until the night and I were one. When I stopped, it was at a pay phone outside a variety store.

"Hello?'

"It's me, Kelly."

"Jane, where are you? I've been phoning."

"Don't. Don't ever again."

"What?"

"I know about the gloves you wore that night, Kelly. So do the police. Do yourself a favour, get rid of that knife you have. The police are going to issue a warrant for your arrest."

"Shit. Jane, I didn't kill my brother. You have to believe me."

"I don't know what to believe anymore. What I do know is that you haven't been honest with me, and that endangers my career and Chrissy's future. Stay away from me."

"Jane, I never–"

I hung up, sobbing now. Damn her.

Damn her to Hell. That place where your heart burns with passion's regret and the brimstone of disillusionment scalds your mind. That place where the sulphur stink of treachery burns your lungs and the flames of anger eat at your soul. I was there, and I wanted her there, too. I wanted her to hurt as much as I did. Did she?

I got through the week on anger and self pity. Gino was terrific. I avoided my parents, taking Chrissy to stay with my in-laws instead. I didn't want to deal with the I-told-you-so. Kelly tried to contact me, but I refused to talk to her. With Chrissy, I laughed and played; alone, I paced and cried. Rejection is emotional rape. I felt violated, ruined for another. I felt shame and anger. I felt like hell.

A week later, I phoned the RCMP recruiting office and asked for application forms to be mailed to me. I phoned Tracy out west on Vancouver Island.

"Hi, Tracy, it's Jane."

"Jane! How wonderful to hear from you. It's been pouring rain for three days. If it doesn't stop raining soon, I'll be talking to the wallpaper. Jane? Jane what's the matter?"

I told her everything. She listened and said little. When I got to the part about retraining for the RCMP and moving west, I could almost feel her hug.

"You can come home anytime you want, Jane, and stay forever if you like. You know you are loved here, and I will make you welcome."

It was what I needed to hear. I did have a place where it was safe to be me and where I was loved. I knew I was not going to get over Kelly easily, but now I felt on firmer ground. I felt I could go on, no matter how painfully.

Kelly was arrested a few days later. That time was the hardest for me. I wanted to be there for Kelly, but I had done all I could for her already. Perhaps if I hadn't had Chrissy, I would have been bolder, but as it was, I kept my distance, pretending that the arrest did not matter to me. It did matter. It mattered a whole lot. I couldn't imagine someone as vibrant and alive as Kelly being behind bars. I worried about her mother and aunt. Who would care for them? Should I phone? I danced around the issues, the master of the double shuffle.

I guess I had always imagined myself as a fairly strong person, someone who would be there for a friend no matter what. I always thought I would uphold the law, taking the high road in every situation. Well, I hadn't. I'd left Kelly to deal with her arrest alone, and I'd compromised my position as a police officer by warning Kelly of her impending arrest.

I have friends who could justify anything, who could simply say, "Well, things changed; it's not my fault or responsibility"; or, "How was I to know?" It was a skill that both impressed and frustrated me.

I tried to justify my actions. I told myself that Kelly had lied to me. I told myself if Kelly was innocent that the courts would rule in her favour. I knew that she would have access to the best defence team. She didn't need me. I told myself all this, but I didn't believe it. Self delusion was not one of my stronger talents. I faulted in my steps, my dance no longer in time to the music I faced.

I had only known Kelly a short time, but I did know she was a very vulnerable person and she would need me. I knew innocent people did end up in jail when fuckers like Heinlein have closed their minds to other possibilities. And I knew that Kelly might have had a rich father, but she didn't have a lot of money for a good defence team. Still, I couldn't pick up that phone and call her family. I couldn't. I was scared.

For two days and nights, I was a wreck. Then, on the third day, Kelly was released from the stony walls of her prison. Her walking was front page news. I spread the paper on the kitchen table and read the text with religious devotion. New evidence indicated that a third party might have been involved in the death of Jason Li. Witnesses had come forth. I waited for Kelly's phone call. It didn't come. I phoned. No one answered. There would be no rebirth of our relationship. I had been the doubter, the betrayer. I had been scared. How I hated myself for my weakness.

The Golden Mountain Crumbles

Jane's call was a double shotgun blast. My insides exploded with fear, and my energy drained in all directions at once. I had no guts to go on. My form didn't move; my only connection with the world was the dial tone repeating in my ear. Jane had left me and I was going to be arrested for murder. The whimpering I heard was me.

I clumsily cradled the phone and ran to the bedroom, tossing the sheets back and throwing the pillows clear as I desperately looked for the knife. What was familiar to me was made invisible by my blind fear. Only when the knife thumped to the floor did I see it.

I grabbed it up and took it to the kitchen and washed it clean. Clean of what? Perhaps of guilt, perhaps of dreams of revenge. Were my lies impaled on its point? I dried it carefully and placed it in the knife block with the others.

My head hurt. The sweat of fear was a stink as strong as death. Jane had left me, but she had pushed me away with the supplies I needed to survive. I needed to think, to be prepared.

How had it come to this? Cast adrift in a sea of trouble, I had chosen neither the ethical nor the moral way. I had chosen instead to lie to myself and to others. There was no going back. I had cut myself adrift from the others, not to save my sister, not to protect my family from shame, but to protect my secret, my shame that Jason had raped me. This wasn't about them; it was about me. I hated myself for being a coward.

Because I couldn't face my own shame, I had hid the truth at all costs. The costs had been very high: my sister's sanity, my father's death, my aunt's hate, my lover's scorn, and now my fall. The Golden Mountain that my father had so carefully built was no more than ice eaten away by the salt tears of secrets and lies.

I sat holding my head and feeling sick as the waves of emotion rocked me back and forth. My wound was deep and gut wrenching. I needed to stem the flow of my fear and bind myself with more lies. I needed to set a course to safety. Coward that I was, I had to save myself.

The night was a long agony of fear and pain. The sun rescued me from my thoughts and I forced myself to work toward my survival. I went to talk to my mother and aunt. The three of us had lived in a frosty coexistence since the deaths of my father and brother. It was difficult to make them understand.

"I need to talk to the two of you."

My aunt folded her arms in stubborn anger.

"Our lawyer say we can not get your father's money until the police say so. Why you no do something about this?"

"It is the law. No one can profit from murder, and so the estate cannot be settled until the police are sure the killer was not someone who would inherit."

"Sarah say Jason killed by an evil spirit. Bad house, she say, built on dragon's eye."

I wiped a hand over my face. "You know better. Jason was killed by a person. Sarah called me after the murder and I went over there and made sure Sarah was safe and that Jason was really dead. Now, because I was there, the police think that I might be the murderer. I want to tell you both that I am not, but there is a good chance that I might be arrested for Jason's murder."

My mother looked shocked. My aunt looked smug.

"You did not kill Jason. I am your mother. I know."

"She killed her father, my husband."

My mother slammed her hand on the table. "I have told you not to talk such rubbish. You have no sense."

I interrupted before the argument continued. "I'll do what I can to set up things so that you are taken care of, but I need you to understand that over the next few weeks, things might get very difficult. Hu, I know, will help you out as much as he can, but he has Sarah and the boys to worry about. I'm worried about the two of you, especially if I am convicted and sent to jail."

The two old women looked at each other. Perhaps they had finally started to realize how serious things were.

"How long you might be in jail?"

"Seven years. Maybe longer."

There was nothing more to say. They knew that the mountain was crumbling around them, too.

My next stop was at my old apartment to talk to Hu.

Hu was shocked, too, but he was smart enough to put things together.

"Sarah called you for help after she killed Jason, didn't she?"

"It doesn't matter what happened, Hu. What matters is that I can trust you to look after Aunt and Mother if I am arrested."

"Of course. It is my honoured duty. But Kelly, you did not kill Jason, did you?"

"No, I didn't."

Hu got up and paced once around the room. I sat quietly, too tired by then to even run on nervous energy.

"I cannot ask you to sacrifice yourself like this."

I blushed. This was not a sacrifice it was a desperate attempt to protect a secret shame. "Hu, Sarah can't handle this and neither can the boys. I need you to be strong and make sure the family is safe and prospers. I'll take my chances."

He looked up and I was surprised to see tears in his eyes. "Sarah loves you very much. You are her hero, you know. She always wanted to be more like you."

This, too, was another shock wave that sent my boat of sanity reeling. "No, I didn't know."

I left after I had explained to Hu what I wanted done and how he could help. I felt numb. For a while, I sat in my car, not knowing what to do. I was now a person without a future – waiting. Drifting. Waiting for either rescue or oblivion. Down deep amongst the bilge water of my life, there was still a pump of hope. I could be strong; I was my sister's hero. I wished I had known before my life was wrecked. Now I did. I was not sure why it made a difference, but it did. I drove back to my mother and aunt's apartment where I was staying.

Over the next few days, I tried to contact Jane, but she never answered the phone. I wanted to go to her house, but I was afraid that my appearance might cause a problem for her. I was not welcomed at work anymore, and my family was uneasy around me. I felt unclean, an outcast of society. My pending misfortune was seen by others as a plague; no one wanted to be too close.

A silly nursery rhyme kept running through my head. *Ring around the rosy, pocketful of posies, husha, husha, we all fall down*. It is a harmless little tune told to children, but I was told once that it was actually the symptoms of the black plague expressed ever so sweetly – the inflamed sores, the wheezing lungs, and the sudden death. It was, or so I was told, a song sung by the dying who would dance around others on the street to infect them. I struggled not to infect others with my problems, but the urge was there. Misery does not wish to be alone. I did not wish to be alone. I drifted. I waited. The wait was painful.

Several days later, I was arrested. Heinlein knocked at our door and his team pushed in. I asked for the search and arrest warrants and was presented with both before I was patted down, cuffed, and read my rights.

My mother and aunt were scared. Often my mother had told me the story of her brother. He had been an engineer who had taught at the university in Beijing in China until he was removed by the Red Guard. They came to his house one night and beat him up and dragged him off. His house was searched, and everything left in ruin. He was in jail for over a year, beaten often until he confessed to having been corrupted by capitalist imperialism and begged to be re-educated in the way of Mao's Communism. He spent the next four years on a farm, working in the fish and paddy fields.

My mother said that they found him one day, floating in the flooded field. No one knew why he died. They thought maybe he'd had a heart attack. My mother thought he had died of lack of hope.

"The Red Guard were thugs. They invaded our homes and took away what was good," my mother would say.

I looked into her eyes as the police went through our apartment. She did not see the police, she saw the Red Guard. She saw the violation.

I knew what she would have seen in my eyes then. She would have seen her brother, without hope.

I was taken first to the police station. My prints were taken and I was photographed. After that, I was allowed to phone a criminal lawyer to represent me. Doctor heal thyself. Lawyers call a colleague. I was placed in a small room containing three chairs and a table. A camera was mounted in the corner of the ceiling. It made me feel uncomfortable to be watched. I had been in rooms like this many times before, but representing a client. This side of the table was far colder. I shivered with fear.

It was Heinlein who entered. He brought a uniformed officer with him. This was standard procedure. Always have a witness. Heinlein was all business. He opened up the file containing my statement to the police, then he took out a tape recorder and stated the date, the case file number, and who was present at the interview. I was listed as the suspect. The charge was second degree murder. This surprised me. The police did not feel that there was premeditation. Why?

"Things have changed now, Counsellor. You are no longer a suspect, you have been charged. Have your rights been read to you and do you understand them?"

"Yes."

"Have you been allowed access to council?"

"Yes."

Heinlein leaned back. "Let's talk about Jason. He's like the golden haired boy in the family, right?"

I didn't feel comfortable talking about Jason. I did not want my shame to come out. "He was supposed to be. My father was delighted when he was adopted. He threw a huge banquet. I can remember it, even though I was very young. Unfortunately, he proved to be a great disappointment. He shamed the family with his ways."

"Yet he would have inherited from your father?"

"I'm assuming he would have gotten the bulk of my father's estate, yes. Although I'm sure my father was realistic enough to provide for my aunt and mother. He knew that Jason could not be counted on. To be truthful, I have no idea what is in the will. It was never discussed with me. I don't think there will be all that much. My father owned two buildings, but he always complained about his debts and mortgages and how he worked to make ends meet."

Heinlein snorted. "Your father owned the buildings outright and had lots of other investments, too. He was worth over ten million."

I tried, but no response came out. After a few seconds, I closed my mouth.

"You telling me a smart girl like you didn't know that?"

"No, I didn't. My father did not share his business with the family. He gambled. He always complained about not having any money. Damn it! I worked my way through school. It can't be true."

Heinlein shrugged. "Let's go over a few things about the night of the murder. Your sister called you?"

"Yes."

"And you headed over?"

"Yes."

"You didn't call the police first?"

"No."

"Why not?"

I shrugged. "Fear for my sister, I guess. I just wanted to get there and make sure she was okay."

"Even though there was a murderer there?"

I looked up and met his eyes steadily. "I assumed, correctly, that a murderer would not have allowed her to make a phone call for help or left her alive. Also, if you refer to my statement, you will see I asked my sister if she was alone. She said she was."

"A murderer could have been holding a gun to her head."

"I suppose. It didn't occur to me, probably because I could think of no reason why a murder would want my sister to call me for help."

We were playing cat and mouse. I was the mouse. He wanted to get me talking and make me feel overconfident, in hopes of tripping me up with my rambling. The sweat trickled down my back. It was a dangerous game. It went on and on.

"So, you checked to see if your brother was dead?"

"Yes."

"Didn't that bother you?"

"That it was my brother, no. We were not close. In that it was a murdered human being, yes, very much so. Even with gloves on, it made me sick to my stomach to touch him."

"What?"

"I felt sick touching him."

"What gloves?"

I hoped I had played this scene right. I had practised it since I'd had the call from Jane. "I took the precaution of wearing plastic gloves, of course. I knew I was entering a crime scene and I didn't want to disturb any evidence."

Looking annoyed, Heinlein flipped back through my written statement. "You never mentioned gloves in the statement you made to the police."

"Sorry. It was an oversight. Yes, I was wearing plastic gloves."

I could see the red crawling up his neck. He was pissed. This was the information he thought he could nail me with. *Thank you, Jane.*

"Where are the gloves?"

"I threw up. I told you that. I ripped off the gloves because they had blood and vomit on them and dropped them in the toilet. After I'd finished being sick, I flushed the lot."

"You said there was blood on the gloves."

"Yes."

"How did that get there?"

"I felt Jason's chest to see if there was a heartbeat. I also touched the blood on the rug. I'm not sure why. I guess because it didn't seem like he'd lost a lot of blood and yet he was dead."

"And maybe you rubbed your fingerprints off the handle of the murder weapon?"

"No, I didn't rub my prints off. I didn't stab Jason. I don't know why you have arrested me. You have my statement and you have my sister's. She was attacked and so was Jason."

"Yeah, well there seems to be some holes in your statement, Kelly, so let's just go through it all again."

And we did. We went over it and over it for hours. It wasn't to get information. By then Heinlein knew he'd acted too quickly in arresting me. He was just getting even. He'd hoped the gloves would rip the case open. My providing the information before he could reveal it to me had shot his boat out of the water. I had to caution myself not to get overly confident. I was still in a dangerous situation, but I was feeling less scared.

He might be able to put forward a case that I'd killed Jason, but not that I'd beat up my sister. He could argue that Jason attacked Sarah and I had come to her rescue and had murdered Jason and then tried to cover up, but it would be hard to make that hold up in court. My car had been noted in my parking space late that night. My defence would easily argue that I didn't have time to murder Jason and cover my tracks before I called the police. Jane had given me the knowledge to help me escape Heinlein's trap.

Nor could Heinlein easily pin the crime on Sarah. She had been attacked. Someone had broken in the back door. She had no blood on her and her prints were not on the weapon. Nor could she be questioned in her present state.

It was the early hours of the morning when Heinlein was finally finished with me. I was taken down to the holding cells. There I was asked to empty out all my pockets and remove any jewellery. My articles were listed, put in a bag and sealed, and I signed. Then I was asked to undress and shower, and a woman officer checked my orifices for smuggled items. Layer by layer, I was slowly stripped of who I was until there was nothing left but a hard grain. Once I was a successful, young lawyer, part of a family and a community. Now I was caged like an animal. My world was stripped of colour: grey blanket, black cot, white toilet, grey brick walls. Time stopped. Life stopped. I sat. I waited.

Once when I was a little girl, I climbed up into the back of a delivery truck that was dropping off bags of rice at my parents' restaurant. The inside smelt of mould and hemp and the exhaust of the road. I felt like an adventurer exploring deep into a cave as I climbed and wove my way through the items to the front of the container. Then the doors closed with a bang and everything went black.

Even now, in recalling that moment, I can feel the terror. I screamed. I pounded on the walls, but the only response was the sounds of the city and road. I bounced about as my earthquake world vibrated, jerked, and swayed.

There was no reason, just blind panic. It seemed like ages, when it reality I had been trapped inside for only a few blocks before the delivery truck pulled up to its next stop. With a clang, the doors opened, and I was blinded by white light. I was lifted, rigid with fear, from my prison and my mother was called to pick me up.

In prison, I felt again like I was confined in the back of that truck. My life has been closed off from me and the course of my life had run out of my control. I rarely cry, but there, in the confines of my cell that first day, I sobbed in fear as I had as a child.

My lawyer visited me. He was optimistic. I was a high profile case and he stood to make good money. He would get me off, he assured me. I understood him. My case would help to establish his career. He didn't ask me if I was guilty or innocent. He didn't care. His job was simple: to defend and win. Law is blind.

During my recreational time, I phoned my mother. There was no answer. I phoned Hu. There was no answer there, either. I had to hope that everything was okay. I hoped, but I worried.

Except for these small interludes and my meals, I was alone. Time was a mountain weighing me down, burying me in doubts. I tried to keep my hope, but hope was the Impossible Mountain. The Soul Lost Mountain. The Golden Mountain of the Li's was in ruin.

Three days and three nights was a long time to think. It was a spiritual eternity without hope. The cross I had borne had been the guilt of my lies told for what I had thought was the greater good. Found wanting, people had lost faith in me. I waited for a miracle. They waited. Time paced slowly with me back and forth, tick, tock, tick, tock.

I had never believed in love at first sight. It was really just need and passion. Some attractions find love later. It is really contentment, and if they are lucky, friendship too. Yet, if I was honest with myself, I would have had to admit that I loved Jane and Chrissy. You couldn't love the one without the other; they were a team. My thoughts drifted back to the crush I had on the schoolgirl on the bus and the pain I felt when I saw her hug her boyfriend at the bus stop. The pain was not as sharp as then, yet it went far deeper in adulthood. Losing Jane was a far greater loss than my freedom. Losing Jane was losing the chance not to be one.

No one wants to be one. For heterosexuals, finding love is hit and miss, but usually successful in the end. For homosexuals and lesbians, it is much harder. Harder to find someone, and harder to keep someone. No one is without scars from the past that they bring to a relationship, but for us they are often still open wounds. Society throws heterosexuals together. Homosexuals and lesbians are pulled apart by society's distain.

I'd had relationships. Jane had not been a relationship; she had been the beginning of love. She had been my chance at happiness, my chance at throwing off my oneness. Could there be another? Maybe. I didn't want another. I wanted Jane.

I imagined the women in the *Titanic* lifeboats. Their loved ones had kissed them good-bye and handed them over to the sailors to be put safely in the lifeboat. Jane had tried to do the same for me. I had to accept that she was saying good-bye forever, but she had placed me in a lifeboat with the information she had shared with me. No matter what, I had to get through the darkness, because that was what Jane wanted for me. I had to keep my hope. I had to accept that I had lost love, but I could still have life. It was painfully hard.

Then there was my father. He was the urban legend that the *Titanic* was unsinkable. He led us all astray. He'd had millions, and pretended all those years that he was struggling to build a small mountain for his family. He sank our dreams with his deceptions. Had Jason known he was rich? It seemed unlikely; otherwise Jason would have probably killed my father. Sitting there in the cell, I realized that I was angry enough to want to murder my father.

Then I laughed, remembering that, according to my aunt, I *had* killed him. It was ironic, like the sinking of the unsinkable ship. I had killed him with honesty. I laughed harder. His life was lies and his death was by the arrow of honesty. I laughed until my tears became sobs, but I held on to the hope.

Another's Darkness

Prison is like a black pearl. We cherish it as valuable, but not so much that we think it is a pure as gold. Prison is black layers of walls and within, the irritants of society. The bigger the irritant, the more the layers of darkness secreted around it. We dress justice up in finery and pretend that the evil within can't escape.

My luminescent pearl, my Kelly, had transformed before my eyes and was now within that dark sphere. I wanted to bury our history within the warm, wet meat and close the shell on our past. I wanted to forget. But I couldn't. I kept diving to the memories, pulling them up and prying open those moments. I was giddy from the depths of our short relationship and couldn't think clearly. I had fallen overboard for Kelly.

I danced around issues with my family, friends, and colleagues for the next few days. It was an exhausting dance, to the sad beat of a dirge. It was finally Gino who insisted that I sit one out and listen to what he had to say. As always, it was in the squad car while we patrolled that the heart to heart took place.

"Squirt, we gotta talk."

"No."

"Yes. The rumour upstairs is that Heinlein has got something smelly on his shoe."

"What?" I was interested now, focused on what Gino was saying. Gino was smart, and cautious about information he heard, and he had friends and relatives in places where good information could be found. If Gino had heard something and was talking, it was worth listening to.

"Word has it the Chief feels Heinlein's case against Kelly Li is unravelling. The Chief is afraid this one could get the department a bad name. If they can't make a case against Kelly, human rights groups are going to be screaming the department is homophobic and racist. He's got the wind up him on this one, and he is leaning on Heinlein pretty hard. Turns out the plastic gloves in the toilet isn't all that great a bit of evidence after all, and word has it that Kelly's lawyer has got witnesses and data to prove Jason Li's death was a mob hit."

I stared at him. "You mean Kelly didn't do it?"

"Didn't say that, Squirt. I said that the police can't make a case against her and chances are she'll be walking soon. I just thought you should know ahead of time."

I nodded and fought back the tears. Gino was good with crying women, but not ones in uniform. He drew the line there. I waited until I had my emotions under control, then asked my question. "Gino, do you think Kelly killed her brother?"

"No. My money would be on the sister, but I tell you one thing, Squirt, Kelly is in deep somehow. You just be cautious. Think with your head, not your heart on this one."

I nodded.

I found out later, when I read the newspaper, that Kelly had been released because of new evidence that indicated that Jason's death might have been related to his heavy gambling debts and his inability to pay.

I waited for her call. It never came.

I picked up my phone many times to call her, but couldn't. It was over. The tides of events had swept away our opportunity. I felt beached. Gritty. Dried in the sun in the stink of mistrust. There was no going back to that tidal pool of emotion, no tasting the salt sea of passion. It was over. I was at a low tide: quiet, weak, revealed.

My family sent my brother Carl to talk to me. Carl, the son, the chosen accountant. He was nervous, repeatedly pushing his glasses up on the bridge of his nose. We look much alike. On me, the features look strong yet pleasant. On him, they look weak and too small for his face. Our gender difference had not fairly reflected our shared genes.

"Mom and Dad are worried about you, Jane."

I twisted the caps on two Molson Canadian. The brew foamed out like spunk. I turned and handed him one of the bottles by the neck. He preferred a glass, I knew. I had no reason to make him feel welcome. I didn't ask him to sit. Instead, I leaned against the kitchen sink and waited for him to do the talking.

"Well, you know."

I waited.

His Adam's apple went up and down and he tried again. "Look, I'm no prude."

I smiled. "No, you're an accountant."

His face darkened. He hated it when I made fun of him. He would never admit it, but he thinks he should have been the cop and I should have been a bookkeeper. Not an accountant, mind you, a bookkeeper. I love my brother, but Carl would have made a poor cop. He lacked the balls, as Gino would say. Balls are not gender related with Gino. He thinks they sprout when you put it on the line for your partner. It's not that Carl was a coward, it's just that he thought like an accountant – slow and conservatively. He wouldn't be there for his partner. No balls.

I had learned that I do have balls, so I didn't cut Carl any slack.

Guys don't.

"Damn it, Jane! You know what I mean. You are involved with a woman again."

I raised an eyebrow. "Your point?"

"The Bible clearly states that sort of behaviour is an abomination before God."

"Leviticus chapter 18 verse 22. Yes, I know. It has become Christianity's rallying cry. Have you read Leviticus, Carl?"

"Well, no. But I know that is what it says."

"You should read it and find out what else it says. The Church is pretty selective in the verses it chooses to reinforce. If it wasn't such an old and respected institution, one might be inclined to say the selective sight of Christians borders on bigotry, if not hate. But what do I know? I'm only an abomination."

"I didn't say that. I'm just reminding you that it's a sin and you should resist it like any other sin. That's what God wants you to do."

"Really? You know this, do you? Had a little man to man talk with Him one night, did you?"

He looked indignant. Indignant and accounting are what my brother does best. "I pray, if that is what you mean."

"I suppose it could have been God you heard, or your own pompous, narrow-mindedness echoing back at you."

"It says in the Bible—"

I rolled my eyes. "I prefer the New Testament, because that is what Christianity is about. My favourite verse is John chapter 14 verse 6: 'I am the Way, and the Truth, and the Life; no man cometh unto the Father, but by Me.' Not by Leviticus, Carl, but by Christ's way. You find me the verse where Christ sees me as an abomination. There isn't one, because Christ's life was about love and acceptance."

"This is so like you – to distort things into the way you want them. With you, everything is misty grey, when life is really black and white. It's the law. You should be able to respect that."

"Respect? Yes. Follow blindly? No. You see, Carl, I decided long ago that it wasn't the Church's interpretations of the faith that were important, but the seeking of the Way through Christ's message of love."

I almost felt sorry for Carl then. He was blinking back tears, because in his own distorted way he did love me. "The Church loves you, Jane. They want to help you."

I gave Carl a hug as I herded him to the door. "No, Carl, the Church doesn't love me, a gay woman. They want to make me over into what they think I should be. They want to pray with me, to help me overcome the terrible infliction they think I have. That's not love, that's a very sick, abusive form of hate."

"Jane, think of your family, your daughter."

"I am. I want Chrissy to be proud of me, the real me. I want her to be open and accepting. You tell Mom and Dad that I'm going to be moving west, so they won't have to worry about any gossip about their dyke daughter at the bridge club. As for my soul, I'll take my chances with a God who judges me for what I am and not who I sleep with."

It felt good to close the door on my brother. I was closing the door on a white bread and mayonnaise world. I might have lost my chance of living in the colourful world that Kelly had brought to my life, but I could lift the paint brush of personal freedom and respect and paint my new life in the rainbow colours of my soul. I was going out west. I was coming out west. I was coming out.

My best friend Brenda was shocked, as if our childhood together might result in her contracting, later in life, a lesbian virus that would ruin her marriage and alienate her children from her. I'd invited her over on an afternoon off. Her children were at pre-school and Chrissy was having her nap.

"A lesbian? You're joking right?"

"No."

"You can't be. I've known you all my life."

"Apparently not."

"You were married. You had a child. Lesbians don't do that. They can't."

I laughed. It came from nerves more than humour. "We have all the parts, Bren. Many lesbian women, like me, get pressured by family and society into living a straight life. It seems easier."

"But, you and Chris, you were so happy together."

I looked at my cup, trying to find the words to help Bren to understand. "Chris knew. I was very honest with him. He didn't care. He thought we were a good pair and could be happy together. In a way, we were. He was my closest friend. I loved him and he loved me, but the passion wasn't there for me. It never was."

"It's probably some hormone thing after the baby. Maybe you should see a doctor. I'll go with you."

I reached out and patted her hand and she pulled away instinctively, then blushed when she realized what she has done. "Brenda, I don't want to be cured. I don't think I'm sick. I want to be a lesbian. It feels right to me."

There was panic in Bren's eyes. "You aren't going to come out of the closet, are you? I mean, everyone knows I'm your best friend! What would my Frank say? You know how macho he is. I mean, what would the guys at his factory say about me?"

"Bren, don't worry. I'm not about to come out. My family feels like you do, and I have no desire to embarrass or hurt anyone. Then again, I am not about to go on living a lie, either. I've decided to do something that I should have done years ago, and that is move out west. I have always wanted to, but my family and friends were here. But now that I know that my family and friends can't deal with who I am, I no longer have that tie. I'm free to live my life as I want."

Brenda looked uncomfortable. "Jane, it's not...well I mean..."

I got up. "It's okay, Bren. I can't help being me and you can't help being you. Do me a favour, though, okay? Try to learn tolerance. Then maybe we can be friends again some day."

Anger replaced her embarrassment as she stood. "I don't think so."

I followed her to the door and closed off another part of my past life. I felt no sadness. I felt liberated, like a butterfly emerging from its dead cocoon.

If you were a giant and could pull a tree out of the ground by the roots and shake off all its leaves, you'd find that what is underground looks a lot like the branches that reach for the sky. A tree is a mirror image, half living in the sun and half living in the dirty side of life. That was how I felt during this time. There were lots of dirty jobs to do, lots of roots to pull free. Some made me angry, some sad, but overall I felt liberated. I unfolded in the sunlight, surprised at how tight a bud I had been all these years.

My support came from the source I least expected, Chris's parents. I had gone to pick up Chrissy and they met me with worried faces and had me come in and sit down. I felt ice form in my gut. I knew without being told that my mother had tried to recruit their support. My mother-in-law delivered the confirmation with my tea.

"Your mother phoned, Jane."

"Oh."

"She asked us to talk to you about your friendship with this woman and your decision to move west."

I said nothing. What could I say? I had lived a lie with their son. I saw my in-laws look at each other and I braced myself for the worst.

"I had to be firm with your mother, I'm afraid. I simply was not prepared to listen to the rubbish your mother was spouting."

I couldn't let her go on. I interrupted. "Bonnie, Tom, it's true. I am a lesbian."

Tom reached over from where he sat on the arm of his wife's chair and patted my knee. "Yes, we know. We've always known. Chris discussed the situation with us before he proposed."

"What?"

Bonnie laughed. "He felt we should know. I must say, at the

time we had concerns about the marriage, but Chris never had a moment's doubt. Men are like that, so tunnel-visioned. We were concerned that Chris might be forcing you into a situation that you would regret. I don't know if you did or not, but I do know that you made Chris very happy and thanks to you, we have Chrissy."

"You knew. I thought... I mean, I thought you'd be upset."

"Only with your parents and brother. I can't say that Tom and I really understand your preferences, but we don't feel that it is for us to judge. Quite frankly, I have no idea why people are so threatened by the issue."

I cried then. They hovered around me, giving me the love and acceptance that I hadn't found with my own family. Their love, their understanding gave me back a bit of what I had shared with Chris.

It was later the question I had been waiting for was asked. It was not asked with anger, though, just gentle curiosity. "Why did you marry our son?"

I fought for emotional control. I wanted to be honest. "Social pressure, I guess, played a part, and my own fear of coming out. But mostly, it was because of Chris. I had dated men, but there had never been anyone like Chris. He was special and I loved him. It wasn't the sort of love that I could feel for a woman, but it was love, and it was friendship, and it was deep and loyal."

Bonnie gave me a hug. "I know that. You two were good together. But we want you to know that we accept the fact that there might be another in your life someday. As long as that person is a good partner and a good parent to Chrissy, you will have our full support whether that partner is male or female."

I held on tight to her. I had no words. My life had shifted. I felt that Chris had reached out from the grave and gently pushed me into the embrace of his family. Chris. I loved him. I always would.

Their Story Part 3

My mother and aunt had been so poor and without hope. The Golden Mountain had given them hope. They had worked hard and had been rewarded. The rewards did not outweigh the pain and sorrow in their lives, but it helped heal the wounds.

They were pragmatic women who expected little and grimly held on to life. They did not talk of love or happiness; they talked of sale prices and good Joss at bingo. They knew life was smoke. They knew how to be smoke and travel safely on the wind. They knew how to survive.

Yin and Yang. Good times/bad times. It was all the same: grey smoke swirling from white to black to white again.

After my arrest, mother and aunt had talked. I never knew what was said, but I imagine it was an agonizing talk. It must have dredged up old, painful history between them, filled with jealousy, competition, insecurity, and pain. They had been rivals all their lives, fighting for my father's favour to maintain their positions within the house. In the end, neither had won. Neither had produced a boy child. Instead, each had accepted defeat at the hands of a stranger who had her son kidnapped one day on a back street in China.

Whatever had been said during those talks, the conclusions were practical. They could only survive by working together and supporting each other. For years, their rivalry had been covered by a thin veneer of friendship, but everything had changed with the passing of my father. They had to allow the conflict below to dissipate and allow the trust and friendship to grow. Mother and aunt could only survive if they had each other, and if they had me. They were far from their culture and ways. Their bridge between the two worlds was me.

They plotted and planned. They didn't hurry. Haste with life would not be respectful to my father's memory. Quietly, they gathered the papers, the witnesses, and times. They had been raised on bureaucracy and interrogation. Their fear was not the process, but the people who operated it. They didn't want to deal with the police. They feared them, but they feared the future more.

So, the two of them dressed in their best clothes and pulled their winter coats close around them. They hired a taxi and went to see my lawyer. They didn't make an appointment. They sat in his office, faces stern and unmovable, bodies bundled and still. They sat until they were given an appointment because they would not go away.

I am sure that my lawyer expected tears and bewilderment. Instead, he was given the key to his success. With determination, my mother presented the defence that she and my aunt had built brick by brick.

"Here are the cancelled cheques we found. Add them up, it is over fifty thousand dollars. Perhaps there were more. We do not know. We know Jimmy Li paid Jason's gambling debts to protect Jason. Here is the proof.

"This man, Hann, he would come and threaten Jimmy. He would tell Jimmy that Jason would have an accident or that bad Joss would come to Jimmy's buildings if he did not pay Jason's debts. Always, Jimmy was angry after. He told Jason he would not continue to pay. Look at this paper. Jimmy Li increased the insurance on his business and our apartment. He was afraid.

"You talk to our neighbour, Lai. He will tell you he saw Hann come to our building many times. He will tell you that Hann ask you if you see if you wish to gamble. Why else would Hann come to our building? He came for money. Jimmy Li would not give him money no more.

"Now we tell you what we know. Hann came the day before Jason died and talked to Jimmy Li in his office. Jimmy said he would not pay Jason's debts no more. He tell this to his wife when she brought him green tea to settle his liver. The liver makes you angry. Green tea is good for the liver. Later, Jason came to see Jimmy Li and they argued. We were glad. Jason was no good.

"Maybe Jason went to get money from Sarah. Jason was stupid. Sarah had a house and sons; there was no money to spare. Jason should have gone to Kelly, but Kelly scared him. Kelly is smart and she is a lawyer.

"Jason could not pay his debts. Someone killed him. Kelly did not kill Jason. Sarah did not kill Jason. Gambling killed Jason. Jason was no good. He shamed his father who gave him everything. Bad things happen at Sarah's house. It is built on the eye of a dragon."

So they unfolded their story. They were pragmatic women. They knew that truth is smoke. Their story was good. It was a form of truth, but truth was not their main concern. Truth would not help them survive. Truth is a luxury.

When my lawyer presented the information to the Crown, I was released. The Crown's case, Heinlein's case, had fallen apart. They didn't want to go to court and lose. They didn't want trouble with the Chinese community.

I was not handcuffed when I left my cell this time. I was taken to a room to change into my street clothes, and then to another to talk to my lawyer. I said little, although I had many questions. I didn't really understand yet why I was being released so suddenly. I listened, but I didn't speak. I didn't want to set a trap for myself with my words.

My lawyer came with me. After some paperwork, I was released into the main entrance lobby of the jail. It was not the one by which I entered. It had no bars. It was solid and gothic and echoed with the footfalls of the outside world. My mother and aunt sat side by side on a wood bench, waiting. When they saw me, they stood. I went to them and hugged each one in turn.

"I know I am free in part thanks to you. You two never cease to amaze me."

My mother nodded. "You come, Kelly. We go home now."

My aunt patted me on the back reassuringly and smiled at me with a toothless grin. She didn't like wearing her dental plate and only did so on special occasions. Going to the prison was not such an occasion.

In the taxi, I talked to my family in Mandarin so we could have privacy. "The lawyer was very impressed by you two. He said you both should have been lawyers. He was not sure why you suddenly came forward when you had not cooperated with the police investigation."

My mother snorted in annoyance. "You cannot explain to these people. They have never had to eat nettles."

Decompression

The next few weeks, I felt restless and distracted. My first thought was to phone Jane. I picked up the phone several times to do so, and then put it down again. There were lies between us, barriers that we might never be able to cross. Jane had made it clear that she couldn't be in a relationship like that. I was sure she had felt the same budding of love as I had. Why else had she phoned with information to help me? But it wasn't enough to overcome the distrust.

I felt hollow. Within a vast empty space, my thoughts and pain floated in bubbles of black depression. One would bubble up, and then another, and I would sit for hours staring at nothing.

My life was a void and I hadn't the energy to pick up the shreds of matter and rebuild.

My mother and aunt got on with life. I took them to bingo, bought their lottery tickets, and saw to the paperwork surrounding my father's estate. In return, they saw I ate and had clean clothes, and planned my day for me. This was the time of my darkness. I had not yet been reborn into this world.

The birth process was long and painful. Spasms of fear and depression crippled me into a ball. When I could, I pushed to be free, but this rebirth was not a journey that could be rushed. I needed to go full term, to deal with the emotions of starting again. It was several weeks later, when I found myself crying for the first time since I left prison, that I knew life had started for me again.

I phoned my old office and talked to my former boss. He was friendly and congratulatory, but I was not asked to come back. What was there to do? I supposed I didn't need to work. My father's estate had left a trust fund that provided a comfortable monthly allowance to both my mother and aunt. My sister and I inherited the remainder, nearly eight million, on the condition that we cared for our mothers.

I was surprised. When I asked about the will, my father's lawyer reluctantly admitted that my father had changed his will nearly a year before his death. Originally, my sister and I were to receive half a million each and Jason the rest. My father had reversed this, leaving a million to Jason, and the rest to my sister and me. With Jason dead, Sarah and I divided the estate between us, except for the two million dollar trust fund that had been set up for mother and aunt.

It was the first time that I grieved for my father. It was not his death I grieved; he had lived a long and good life. I felt instead sorrow, that a year before his death he'd given up on his one dream, to leave his Golden Mountain to a son that would be worthy of his family name. My father was a modern, successful man in many ways, but the old country was still very deep within him. Sarah and I had inherited, not because he saw us as worthy, but because we were the only ones left. In my soul, I knew that I would have gladly given up my inheritance to have my father see that I was worthy of him. He was not capable of that.

How many people have I disappointed in my life? Certainly, my father, who wanted a son, and my mother, who needed a son to legitimize her relationship with my father. There was my employer, who had seen a great future for me before my arrest, and Sarah, who had counted on me to help her and had instead been driven to madness with guilt. And Jane. The woman I loved. The woman who believed in me until I disappointed her, too. This was my lowest point before my rebirth, when the aborting of my life seemed for the best.

My time of darkness was Sarah's awakening. The police, with the exception of Heinlein, I'm sure, now believed that Jason had been killed by an unknown assailant because of his debts. It had said as much in the paper. Sarah and I were no longer suspects. Hu said she had read the article in the paper over and over again.

She came to realize what really had happened. Jason had not attacked her that night; he had only wanted money. Someone had broken in who wanted Jason dead because Jason was no good. Someone who hated Jason.

She had run to get the knife, but she hadn't stabbed Jason. The black dragon had stabbed Jason. The hate had stabbed Jason. She was not guilty. She carried no shame, because none of it ever happened.

I had been right. She didn't remember anything bad happening to her. She hadn't killed Jason. She hadn't been raped by him. None of it happened. Someone broke in, like I had told her. Someone who hated Jason had broken into his chest and ripped out his dark soul. The black dragon.

Gradually, Sarah reclaimed her life. Gradually, her denial became her reality. Sarah had found a way to bury her shame and guilt. She could go on again. Truth is smoke.

I needed to break free from the past, too. Not through denial, but by fleeing. The red walls of my youth had bricked me in for far too long. I needed to be free of this world and of my past. I wanted a new life.

I talked to my mother and aunt. I was honest with them.

"I need to find work some place where people don't know my

past. I want to be free of my father's house."

It was my aunt who responded. "We go west."

My mother nodded. "Many from Chinese Club have moved west. In Vancouver, it is warmer. No bad winter. Many Chinese live in the west. We go. You will buy us a condo there. When we go play cards on Thursday, I will ask where to live."

And so, it was decided for me. I would go west, because the winters were warm and that is where the old of the Chinese community wished to retire. I didn't mind. I didn't care where I lived, as long as it wasn't there within red brick walls.

The West

It took nearly a year to settle my father's estate. My brother's estate was debt that disappeared with his life. His murder was never solved. A few months after my release, Hann was found dead in the Credit River. The newspaper said he might have fallen through the ice. More likely, he leaned on the wrong family. For us, it was good Joss. Hann's icy death made my brother's case cold.

I bought my mother and aunt a two bedroom condominium over looking Vancouver harbour. They liked to drink their afternoon tea on the balcony in the good weather and watch the ferries heading out to the island. They would take a bus to Chinatown, or go to Stanley Park to do Tai Chi in the warm afternoons. Four times a week, they went to the Chinese Centre and played cards or bingo. On Sundays, I would visit them. They were happy.

I was not happy. I existed. I worked toward a new life with steadfast determination. It kept me occupied. I did not wish to think. I did not wish to feel. When the loneliness got too great, I would go to a bar that lesbians frequented. I would drink, listen, and not think. I talked little. I never asked anyone out or invited anyone home. There was no point. I had nothing to give.

I studied for the British Columbia bar exams and got a job working for social services. I bought a house. I took up riding and broke my arm when I fell off. With grim determination, I got back on again. Riding is what women do. This was how I filled five years of my life.

This western exile changed one afternoon in a police station. I was waiting for a client, flipping idly through an RCMP magazine. Then suddenly, there she was, looking back at me from the page – a grainy black and white ghost from my past. Constable Jane Anderson, who had been on the force three and a half years, had received a special commendation for saving the life of a trapped motorist.

I stole the magazine. For weeks I kept it under the pillow of my bed, taking it out to stare at Jane's features while my mind played back the flicking memory newsreel of our relationship. I was a one person audience, watching a tragedy unfold over and over again in the empty theatre of my room. I was still in love with the star. In love with a picture in black and white and the memories. They were a silent movie.

I was an obsessed fan of Constable Jane Anderson. I rooted through police files to find her posting and her address. On weekends, I took the car ferry to Vancouver Island and headed up the coast to spy. I drove past her house and the station where she worked, and cruised her neighbourhood. I discreetly took pictures of all this.

I felt both exhilarated and afraid. I knew I was acting stupidly, irrationally. Yet, I couldn't stop. It was the most alive I had felt in years. Jane was near. I was obsessed.

One Sunday, my mother asked to talk to me. My aunt cleared the table and disappeared into the kitchen. During the first four years in Vancouver, they had moved from competitors to conspirators. Close as sisters.

"You no around on Saturdays never."

"I often go to the island."

"Why you do this?"

I shrugged, annoyed to feel the heat of a blush spreading up my neck. "I like it there."

"There is a woman."

I looked up in surprise. I had always been very discreet. I was shocked that my mother knew my orientation. I didn't lie. "No, not really."

"What does this mean?"

"There is someone on the island I once knew. I have not renewed our friendship."

"The policewoman."

Again I'm shocked. I say nothing.

"You bring her for dinner maybe."

"I'm not seeing her."

"That stupid. Why you go to bars and pick up girls for drink when you could have this nice policewoman for a friend? You crazy."

My face flamed. Someone in the Chinese community must have seen me at the bar. The Chinese community loves gossip. Privacy comes from not acknowledging rather than not knowing.

"It's past history."

"No history is past. Always it comes back. You want to catch AIDS in these bars? No, you ask policewoman to come for dinner."

Now I understood. The two old conspirators were afraid I'd die and leave them to fend for themselves. "I'm not going to catch AIDS. I don't sleep around."

My mother lapsed into disapproving silence and I left shortly after.

For several weeks, I wavered, a wave lapping in and out. Each time getting closer to a decision before retreating again. Finally, on a high tide of need, I headed over to the island to see Jane.

It was not easy facing a ghost. Chrissy was three when I knew them, by now she was closer to eight. I was a stranger. What if Jane had another partner? That thought, I refused to consider. It was too painful.

Once there, my nerve left me. I couldn't bring myself to knock on the door. *Knock, knock.*

Who is there? It was just too hideous to consider. I stopped and pumped gas into my car's tank as a delay technique. Gas on the island was expensive. It was cheaper, though, than the cost of embarrassing myself. Inside the station, I paid the attendant.

"Do you know if Mrs. Jane Anderson lives around here?"

"Constable Anderson?"

"Yes."

"Sure. Her and her daughter live with Tracy up on her spread the other side of Campbell River. Just follow the road west and look for a sign that says Stone River Farm. It's a nice place they got out there."

I managed to smile and nod, I think, as I fumbled my change and somehow managed to get back to my car. Jane was living with a woman. Denial had prevented me from facing such a logical possibility. Now reality was staring me in the face and I feared it. I sat for a long time trying to pull myself together, and then headed back to the mainland. Standing on the car ferry heading back to Vancouver, I watched the island retreat, watched my dreams diminish. Jane was water under the bridge, the past. I was a fool to think that I could change the flow of events.

Her West

The West. How many have moved toward the sunset hoping for a better life? I packed the U-Haul, the lesbian chuckwagon, and headed west. It was a great adventure in the eighteen hundreds and now. It was also very difficult both then and now.

Thank God for Tracy! She was there for me and Chrissy. She had hugs for us both and wiped our tears. She was mother, confessor, and friend. Through her, I had my Aunt Edith back. Aunt Edith-of-the-West, who understood and made every day an adventure.

Tracy lived on the old spread. It was forty acres in the interior of Vancouver Island. The house was an old two storey clapboard built at the turn of the century. There was an old log barn, a modern tool shed, and a long lean-to used as a garage. Not picture perfect by any means, but warm and inviting.

It was home. I had known that from the first time I visited it when Cleo was still alive, but then there were ties that pulled me back to Ontario. The ties were severed now and I had found my place – Jane-of-the-West.

The land was magical. To the west, mountains rose green against the sky and forest barricaded the northern winds, and to the east and west, farms met up with the Stone River property. Stone River was more of a big creek. It ambled across the rolling pastureland in a slow curve. In the spring, the fields were a mass of wildflowers and in the summer, our horses grazed on the sweet grass. The fall turned the aspens gold, and in the winter, the deer and birds came to the feeding stations we set up.

Chrissy was happy; I was not. I existed. I retrained as a Mountie and was lucky to be posted to the island. When I wasn't working, I helped around the ranch, tending the horses, weeding in our kitchen garden, and helping with repairs. Sometimes Tracy's friends dropped over and formed a grey haired knot around the kitchen table. They were liberated women from the sixties, hippies who had morphed into gay women. Chrissy brought school friends around, too. They would help in the barn and then ride around the paddock on our three old quarter horses. Glue-horses, Tracy called them, because she said had she not bought them, they would have been sent to the glue factory. They were called Stuck-up, Paste, and Crazy-glue. Crazy was my horse. I rode her a lot in the evenings.

Tracy stirred a pot of homemade soup on the big range. I sat at the kitchen table chopping carrots.

"You should call her."

"Who?"

"Kelly."

My heart thumped in my chest. "Don't be silly. That's water under the bridge. It's been two years."

"Water keeps on running all the way to the sea and so have you. You are never going to be happy until you have some resolution, one way or the other."

"I'm happy."

"Sure you are. Here, give me those carrots and cut up some of the celery stalks now."

"She's probably found someone else and got her life back together. She's a really good lawyer."

"So you said. So, if it's over, why haven't you found someone else instead of hanging around with my old friends and me?"

"I've been busy – my new job, Chrissy, you know."

"I know. That's why I'm asking, why don't you phone her?"

But I didn't, not then and not later. I wanted to, but I couldn't. I hadn't been there for her when she had needed me. I'd doubted. Instead, I'd taken Chrissy and run. How many pioneers had done the same? Run. Run from persecution, poverty, trouble, and pain. To what? To hardship. How many were happy? How many never found resolution?

Aunt Edith and Cleo are buried side by side on the property. It's an old pioneer graveyard on a small hill. On a clear day, to the east you can see the water of the Strait of Georgia. Tracy wants to be buried there too. Maybe I will be someday. Proud, strong women all. Could I earn the right to lay with them?

The RCMP is like most police services on the surface, but underneath there is this sense of tradition. Pride. They represent the nation. They are part of Canada's history. They were the first red root of justice. Like all forces, a rookie has to prove their worth. Because I was a woman, I had to prove myself as an officer and as a person. For the first year, I felt isolated. I was not one of the team, but someone who simply worked for them. On duty, I was alone in my squad car, and in the office I was ignored after polite hellos.

My chance to grow balls came when I responded with other officers to a hostage taking. An unemployed lumber worker had locked himself in the house with his ex-wife and two-year-old daughter. Our domestic crisis officer made contact and talked for hours. No good.

At three in the morning, as I sipped coffee by the police emergency van, my sergeant came up to me. "Anderson, your record shows you as being a pretty good marksman."

"Yes."

"Could you take him out?"

I swallowed. This was a situation no cop wants to be in. "If I have to."

He nodded. He understood. "Crisis management say he's rigged a bomb and has it strapped to his little girl. Can you imagine that? They think he's just playing with us all and that he means to do it no matter what we do. Get ready. There might only be one chance. If an opportunity arises, take it."

"Yes, sir."

My voice sounded calm. Inside, I was a mess. I went and got a sniper rifle from the support truck. Automatically, I went through the routine I had been taught. I separated my actions from my being. I tried not to think. Thoughts would only lead to indecision.

The other officers watched in surprise. They were surprised that a rookie had been asked to make the kill. They were more surprised that rookie was a woman. Another pressure. If a man missed the shot, it would be bad luck. If a woman missed, it would be because women haven't got what it takes. I read once that during World War II, the Russians trained women as snipers. They were more patient and accurate, their hit rate much higher than men's. I tried to find out more about them, but their story had never been told. They were only women.

Sometimes you do it right. It's a gut thing. Instead of taking my position, I went and talked to them in the crisis wagon first.

"Try to get him to talk about the bomb. I want to know how he detonates it. If you make him feel he is pretty smart for being able to make one, he might describe it," I suggested.

I took my place then, lying on my stomach on the roof of a van. The bank of police lights concealed me. I waited. Some hours later, my earpiece cracked with static. I was told the bomb's structure. Maybe, just maybe I could get him before he killed anyone.

I had watched him through the curtains of a side window. The three of them were crouched in a corner. He talked on a cell phone to the police. I saw them as if in a dream through the white lace of respectability. Despite the bulky bomb tied on her small chest, the small child slept in the arms of her frightened mother. The woman was cut, bruised, and bleeding.

It all happened at once.

"He's going to do it!" someone screamed through my earpiece. I saw him scramble angrily to his feet and turn to drag the woman up. I squeezed the trigger.

"Go!" I yelled, and the Special Force charged forward. The door slammed open and the room filled with the black flak jackets of cops. Carefully, I took out the rifle's magazine and slid along the roof. Shaking, I half climbed, half fell down the ladder at the back of the van. No one was watching. The heroes were inside, under the glare of the floods, rescuing the mother and child. I covered the rifle with my jacket and stowed it away in an evidence box as quickly as I could. I didn't want to be seen with it.

The man didn't die. My bullet had torn through his left lung and missed his heart by inches. I'd been lucky. The woman and child had been lucky, too. The man would never be lucky. He was born to be a loser.

Nothing was said about my role that night, but things changed. Now I was one of the boys. I had balls.

That night changed me, too, just like the night Chris was killed changed me. I placed a picture of Kelly that I had kept hidden in my drawer in a frame by my bed and made sure that I reminded Chrissy about her Chinese-Canadian aunt. I asked Tracy to be Chrissy's guardian.

"I'm too old."

"No you're not. Chrissy loves you."

"Do you think?"

"I know."

And so it was done. I was content again, but not happy.

My Loss. My Rescue.

Several weeks went by after my last trip to Vancouver Island. I dealt with my loneliness and disappointment by developing a cold. After ignoring it for several weeks, it became pneumonia, a testament to my neglect of body and soul. Armed with a prescription, I took to my bed with a high fever, feeling only about one degree off truly lousy. My mother and aunt phoned and offered advice and sympathy. They didn't visit. The old fear colds as much as they fear bullets. I slept fretfully, slightly off kilter, waking from nightmares that reduce fever to cold sweat.

It took a while before I realized that the hammering of my headache was augmented by the knocking on the door. I rolled out of bed with a groan and slipped into sweat pants and a top. Blurry eyed and damp with fever I made my way to the door, anticipating yet another order of Chinese medicines that my mother had sent.

It was Jane.

"You're sick."

"It's just pneumonia."

"You've lost weight."

I shrugged. "You look good."

"Are you going to let me in?"

I stepped aside. "Sorry, of course."

She felt my forehead and I got a whiff of her perfume. It reminded me of summer heat and wild flowers. She took off her coat and shoes and got me comfortable on the couch with pillows and a blanket while she changed my bed and made me soup and toast. I was too tired to argue and grateful for her efforts. Satisfied for the time being that she had done all she could, she settled in a chair opposite me.

"You asked about me at the garage."

I blushed. "Yes. I saw your picture in a police magazine and thought I'd look you up. The gas station attendant said you were living with someone, so I didn't want to intrude." I made my voice casual. It was not how I felt. Inside, my levels were off. My thoughts were out of alignment and my headache acute.

"I live with Tracy. She was Cleo's partner after my Aunt Edith died. She is like a grandmother to Chrissy."

I sat up, my world suddenly at right angles again. "I thought... How is Chrissy?"

Jane beamed. "Happy and doing well at school. I told her I was coming over to the mainland to see you. Tracy is taking care of her."

"Chrissy remembers me?"

"I've talked about you." Silence. "I'd better be going so you can get back to bed."

"No! I mean... How did you find me?"

"Stan at the garage got concerned that he'd told you where I lived. The next time I stopped for gas, he gave me a description of you and your licence plate number. I ran it through motor vehicle registration and came up with your name and address."

"Why?"

"Probably for the same reason that you tried to look me up. I've missed you."

I looked up and met her eyes. "When I'm feeling better, we could maybe see each other. You know, go out."

The eyes darkened with intensity. "That depends."

"On what."

"The truth about what happened back then."

"You're still a cop."

"You're still a suspect. We need to get past this."

I looked away. Trust was never easy for me. I had never put the knife back under my pillow, but I imagine it there.

After floating aimlessly for so long, my safe harbour was in sight. I wasn't sure I could handle sharing my voyage. When the *Carpathia* arrived in New York with the survivors of the *Titanic*, the press milled around wanting answers. Each individual had to justify why they were alive while so many were dead. Survivor guilt they call it. You see, they all shared a secret. They had all fought to live. They had all managed to survive, even at the cost of the lives of those closest to them. I had survived. I had kept the secret of my shame close. Jason and my father were dead. My mother and aunt had been uprooted to start yet another life. And my sister Sarah was only happy in the sad world of denial. How did I justify that truth?

I reached out for Jane. I was not sure where our future would take us, but I knew that we would go there together. It would not be easy. Happiness must be won.

Truth

I watched Kelly struggling with the truth. She needed to tell me what really happened that night. It was the only way we could go on. A relationship might have its secrets, but it must always have trust. This was the last dance of the evening. I had cut into Kelly's life and danced close, the rhythm of my hips and the line of my body on hers telling her that our dance was special. The melody of our song was a mixture of east and west. Was the last dance to be mine and would we go home together? I waited.

Then it all came out. With an imaginary knife, Kelly pierced the festering abscess and painfully squeezed the pus out for me to see. I sat with her as the poison of that night leaked from her heart and soul. It was not a police report, it was a detailed cleansing. I was told everything: thoughts, actions, fears, doubts. I knew as I listened that this was trust. This was truth. Kelly was a single survivor of the wreck that was Jason's life. When she was finished, I held her close. Her fever broke during the night, and in the morning I was still there.

And After

Still there. I have to believe that what Kelly and I found in each other was meant to be. Falling in love is easy; staying in love is not. We had to work at it like all couples, but the work was not unpleasant. Unpleasant was the gossip, stares, and remarks that we had to endure, the taunting and laughter that Chrissy sometimes faced. Unfair was a cold autumn dawn.

"Mommy, why did they do that to us? Why don't they like us? We're nice."

"Yes, we are nice. Most people are, but a few are so filled with righteous hate and bigotry that it blinds them to everything but their own narrow, narrow worlds."

"Why do they hate?"

"I don't know, Chrissy. They just feel they are right and so everyone else must be so terribly wrong."

"I don't think what they did was right."

Chrissy was right. Those boys who banged on our door in the early hours of the morning and threw a brick through our window, those boys who filled our mailbox with straw and set it alight, are they godly because they are not gay? The judge gave them a lecture and community service. Are they the sort that should be helping in our community?

The Church became a banner for the homophobic to rally under. Every bigot could then cry gays were sinners and justify a witch hunt. Do people really believe these people are the true followers of Christ's way? Did the Church understand that its opposition to gay rights was a sanction for gay abuse?

Resolution

Jane and I are still together and happy. Chrissy has gone, first off to university and then to work in Hong Kong with her husband. Tracy has gone, too. She lies beside Edith and Cleo. They were a trilogy of truth that helped Jane and me find our way.

Jane's parents were unforgiving and now dead. Carl had them cremated and buried in a huge cemetery in Toronto. Jane visited once. The tombstone was white marble, she told me. It was the last time she visited Carl. He was still sad for her. His wife made small shrimp and mayonnaise sandwiches to go with a chilled white wine. Bread and fishes, but no miracle happened, just life.

Chris's parents are still alive and live close by us in the same condo complex as my aunt. They are old, but still as involved and excited about life as ever. I have enjoyed knowing them.

My mother died not many years ago. Jane and I took a little bit of her ashes back to China and scattered them in the village where she had been born. We have promised to do the same for Aunt Quin.

Jane and I live on the old homestead. We have horses and still ride. Sometimes we take our kayak to the beach and paddle off for a few days to camp on the islands in the channel. I enjoy taking photos of the whales as they migrate. We have gotten old together, grown together like strong tree roots hug the rocky shoreline. The scars and wear marks of life, I think, have made us more beautiful. I am happy in this world of colour. I feel alive.

Jane is happy too. She has come to terms with the past and has learned to see the good that came from it. This is our story, our life. Not so different really from others'. We have recounted it here because today, after twenty years together, we were able to get legally married here in Canada. The family we formed was all there with us for our special day. We stood under the big oak that Jane's Aunt Edith and Cleo planted as a sapling their first year together. They were never able to marry. Neither could Tracy and Cleo. They were couples. They loved each other deeply. But they did not have the same rights as other Canadians.

Married. Two women, one life, under the law. It has been a long climb to the summit of Golden Mountain. But we are there.

Anne enjoys travelling and learning about different cultures. Although retired, she still takes an active interest in archaeology and forensic anthropology. She lives in northern Ontario and enjoys her days in her canoe. Her hobbies include travelling, writing, and painting. You can contact Anne at a_azelca@hotmail.com.

Printed in the United States
64197LVS00005B/202